NEON ZIGGURAT

NEON ZIGGURAT

ANGIE LOFTHOUSE

Also by Angie Lofthouse

Novels

The Glory of the Stars

Defenders of the Covenant

The Ransomed Returning

Short Fiction

Ripped and Other Adventures

Spirits Bright

Joy Ride

To Tracy
For his unwavering support of my crazy dreams.

1.

Span Corp tower loomed over the Los Angeles skyline like a brooding god. A megalithic monstrosity. A monument to the modern age. Garish holographic images paraded around its colossal façade—ads for Span Corp communication products (as if anyone wasn't already using them), music videos, or stunning natural scenery, the sort one just didn't see anymore. Not in L.A. anyway.

Pressley Pierce hunched over her handlebars and pushed her bike faster as she raced through the streets toward the tower. The wind whipped against her cheeks, hot even this early. She'd spent too long this morning bending over her toilet, and she didn't want to be late to work again. Too many more times and she'd get fired. Something she couldn't afford to do, for more reasons than one.

Hazard wants results.

That's what Gil, her recruiter, had told her last night.

Not this penny ante crap you've been sending.

"Sure," she grumbled to herself. Did Gil think she wasn't trying? Did he think Span Corp's system was that easy to crack? Ha. Well, she had something special planned today. If it was dirt on CEO Ransom McCleary that Hazard wanted, that was what he'd get.

Pressley let the bike take the lead, weaving through the thickening traffic on the freeway. She leaned into the rhythm as it swerved between slower-moving vehicles. Her stomach rolled, but she ignored it. She punched the bike forward around a couple of cars to reach her exit. One of them laid on the horn, and Pressley responded with a raised middle finger. She sped through the city streets bustling with cars, buses, more bikes, and people on foot or on scooters or hoverboards. Span Corp Tower loomed ever larger. She cast her eyes upward to the very top where McCleary ruled from his luxury penthouse, looking down on the rest of them like they were his serfs. "I'm coming for you," she whispered. She pulled into the parking garage under the tower and wound downward until she found an open charging stall for her bike.

Her phone jangled in her earpiece—a purple gem on her temple. She pulled the phone from her pocket. It was Twiggy, her baby sister.

"Hey."

"Press, guess what I did last night."

A holographic image of Twiggy hung in the air in front of Pressley, moving with her as she walked across the parking garage.

"Please tell me you didn't go out with that loser again."

"No way." Twiggy shook her head, flapping her pink ponytails around her face, making her look even younger than her eighteen years. "I dumped him a week ago."

"Good. What did you do last night?"

"So, Cherry, my roommate, right?"

Pressley nodded. The smell of rubber and oil and humanity made her even queasier.

"Well, she wanted to go to this beach party last night, and at first, I wasn't going to go because I had a ton of homework. Then Cherry said—"

"Short version, Twig. I'm late for work."

"I got a tattoo!" she squealed, waving her arm in Pressley's face. Pressley flinched as the holo of Twiggy's arm fuzzed and glitched, not helping her stomach.

"Hold it still."

The new tattoo came into focus, a shimmering butterfly that swirled around Twiggy's arm up to her neck, around and down the other arm, where the journey repeated in reverse.

"Wow. That looks—" Expensive, she was going to say, but Twiggy interrupted.

"I know. It's so pretty. You have to see it in person."

"Yes." And they could talk about how a freshman at UCLA could afford a holo-tat that moved around both arms. "Come over tonight," Pressley said. "I'll cook for you."

"I'll be there." Twiggy hung up, and the holo disappeared. Pressley stopped for a second and leaned against a concrete pillar to let her stomach settle before she went inside. One of Span Corp's cyborg enforcers walked by, his black suit stretching over unnaturally enhanced shoulders, and gave her the stink eye. Pressley straightened and headed inside.

◦ ◦ ◦

The elevator ride up to the 121st floor was enough to settle her stomach a bit. She reached her cube and nodded hello to her co-workers, Corny on the right and Deedee on the left. Inside her own little glass box, she turned the walls opaque for more privacy, set them to a soothing nature scene, and booted up her computer.

She answered a couple of emails just in case a supervisor was monitoring her activities. From the pocket of her leather riding jacket, she retrieved a little data siphon, slid open her desk drawer, and deftly swapped out the siphon she'd placed last week with the new one. A tiny green light indicated it was on, her newly programmed bots worming their way ever deeper into Span Corp's system, scraping all the data and returning any interesting bits to the siphon. Today, she'd programmed her bots to scrape more aggressively, to burrow deeper into the system than she'd yet dared to go. Maybe that would get Gil off her back. That done, she turned her attention to her actual job.

◦ ◦ ◦

Three hours later, Pressley lunged for the trash can under her desk, getting it up in the nick of time to empty her stomach into it. When the retching stopped, her head slumped onto the desk. She felt around for her water bottle, knocked it to the floor, and listened to it roll until it thumped against the cubicle partition. She groaned.

Someone tapped a knuckle against the sliding door of her cube. Her coworkers would have to be deaf to have not heard that. "Come in," she muttered without lifting her head.

The door slid quietly open, and Cornelius appeared, a sympathetic smile on his sweet, round face. "Here. This might help." He held out a Coke and a vending machine pack of soda crackers.

"Thanks." She pushed herself up. The stench from the wastebasket wrinkled her nose. "Sorry about that."

Corny scooped up the defiled bag, tied it off, and tossed it toward the sliding door, then settled himself on the edge of her desk. "So, what's up?"

Pressley nibbled the edge of a cracker. "Must have eaten something that disagreed with me." It wasn't the truth, but she wasn't ready to discuss the truth with Corny. Or anyone.

"You've been eating a lot of disagreeable food lately." Corny raised an eyebrow shrewdly.

"Maybe it's a stomach bug." Pressley cracked open the Coke, but the smell of it almost set her off again. She pushed it away.

"So, I'm guessing you didn't get prior authorization for your pregnancy?"

Pressley shook her head, jaw clenched. No use denying what he already knew. Made her wonder what else he might have guessed about her.

"You know you can't keep it, right?" He laid a gentle hand on her shoulder.

"I know." A tiny stab of anger flashed hot in her chest. Who was Span Corp to make that decision for her? But there it was. Termination required for any pregnancy not pre-authorized. Unfair policies like that were just the reason for her data-siphoning.

Corny squeezed her shoulder. "Have you made an appointment yet?"

"Not yet." She nibbled another corner off her cracker. Her stomach roiled. She looked away. "I'll make an appointment today," she told him.

Corny relaxed. "Good girl. It's the best choice, and don't feel bad. It happens. No big deal."

Easy for him to say.

"I'll come with you if you want," Corny continued. "Be your emotional support animal." He smiled.

Pressley nodded. "You're a good friend, Corny. I'll let you know if I need you."

"Okay." Corny stood and scooped up the bag of puke. "I'll take care of this. You take care of you."

"Thanks, Corny." She lifted the cracker in an awkward salute as he left and slid the door shut behind him.

She really should make that appointment. The company healthcare clinic took up the entire twenty-fifth floor. She could get the procedure done and be back in her cube in a couple of hours. It would be the smart thing to do. She laid her head on the desk. Who knew she'd feel so conflicted? She sat up, straightened her chair, and took a tentative sip of the Coke.

Eww. No. She pushed it away again. Back to work, then. She could always make the appointment tomorrow.

◦ ◦ ◦

Twiggy was already in her apartment when Pressley made it home.

"You're late," Twiggy said, taking a sip of her iced latte. The butterfly tat flitted up and down her arms. The frenetic movement made Pressley's head hurt.

She flopped onto the couch, exhausted and sick from the long ride home. "Traffic," she told Twiggy. "Sorry about that."

Her small Span Corp employee apartment was on the tenth floor of a gray brick twelve-story building. A tiny window next to the front door let in the washed-out sunlight and the noise of traffic and drones below, along with the smell of e-cigs and weed. Pressley's stomach almost couldn't take it.

"Would you mind turning off the tat?"

"Oh, yeah. Over-stimmed?" Twiggy tapped the butterfly. It fluttered up under her sleeve and didn't emerge. "I'll probably only turn it on for parties and whatever." It'll help me stand out and get noticed by the right people."

"Great." Twiggy wanted so badly to become an actress, a big-time movie star. Pressley didn't have the heart to tell her that it was nearly impossible, no matter how many acting classes she took or tattoos she got or so-called directors she flirted with. Opportunities like that were so slim as to be non-existent. It hurt Pressley to think of her sister stuck in a dead-end corporate job like she was, with pretty perks but little choice in her life and no options for leaving or changing anything. No legal options, at any rate.

"You look tired," Twiggy said. The understatement of the year. "Want me to cook instead?"

"Yes, please." Pressley stretched out on the couch and covered her eyes with her arm. From the sound of it, Twiggy had pulled out a couple of frozen meals to microwave. She clenched her teeth.

"So," she said when the nausea was back under reasonable control. "Where'd you get the tattoo?"

"From a guy I met at the beach party. He said he does tats for the stars all the time."

"Really?" That seemed doubtful. Pressley forced herself upright again. Twiggy set the warmed dinners out on the counter.

"Yeah, but he wants to get his name out among the general public, too, so I'm supposed to talk it up or whatever."

"I see." She pulled up a barstool next to Twiggy.

"You should get one," Twiggy said. "That would be so cool. I bet I could get you a good discount."

"Maybe." Pressley poked at the gooey lasagna on the cardboard tray. Would a tat like that hurt the baby with its specialized inks and nanite tech? She shuddered. She wasn't keeping the baby, she reminded herself. She couldn't.

And then for some odd reason, her mother popped into her head. Had Mom faced this dilemma with Pressley and then again with Twiggy? Weird how she suddenly wanted to ask her when she hadn't spoken to her mom in several years.

"Do you ever think about Mom?" she asked Twiggy, giving the lasagna another poke.

"What? Ew. No," Twiggy said. "I mean, yeah, but not because I want to." She giggled. "Can you imagine what she'd think of my tat?"

"She'd never let you out of the house again." Even Twiggy's hot pink pigtails or Pressley's purple streaks would have given their mother a heart attack, not to mention Pressley's pregnancy.

"Glad I don't live there anymore." Twiggy pointed her fork at Pressley's untouched meal. "What's wrong? Don't you like it?"

"It's fine." Pressley's stomach flip-flopped. She pushed the tray away. "I'm just not hungry."

○ ○ ○

Three days later, she slumped over her desk. She still hadn't made an appointment at the health center, still hadn't passed the full data siphon to her boyfriend, Bobby, like she should have, still hadn't found anything new. And Gil did not appreciate her responding to his messages with only a middle finger emoji.

Numbly, she stared at the computer screen, not even seeing the piece of code she was supposed to be working on. Maybe if she found something juicy enough with her hacking, Hazard Snow would pay her a bonus or even give her a job or help her find something away from Span Corp. Maybe—

Her phone chirped, and she was instantly alert. That tone meant only one thing. Someone had noticed her hacking. She grabbed her phone to check the app she'd written to keep track of her system infiltration. Looked like she had succeeded in getting farther into the system than she'd ever been. Maybe a little too far.

Shit. She'd caught the attention of the cybersecurity team. She sent the kill order to delete her bots and scrapers as fast as she could, but probably she was already too late. It wouldn't take security long to trace it all back to her.

Seemed she'd be leaving Span Corp, like it or not.

She popped the data siphon off the underside of the desk and grabbed her black leather riding jacket from the hook on the wall. She rapped on Corny's cube wall as she went by. The door stood open. He swiveled around in his chair.

"Cover for me?" Pressley said. "If anyone asks, I'm too sick to stay."

She hurried away, not waiting for his reply.

"You made the appointment?" he called after her.

She waved her hand noncommittally. It pinched her chest a little. Cornelius had been a good friend, and she would miss him. Her phone and earpiece went into the nearest incinerator chute.

The elevator ride from the 121st floor down into the bowels of the parking garage felt like hours. At every floor, she expected it to stop, for the doors to open, and for security to come drag her away. She made it all the way to her bike before she had to puke against a pillar. Yuck. She said a silent apology to the person parked beside her. With another swig from the water bottle to get the taste out of her mouth, she mounted her bike and took off for the entrance.

A few levels up, a figure stepped out between the rows of vehicles and stood in her path, tall and broad, dressed in a black suit. "Pressley Pierce!"" The voice echoed through the garage. A cyborg enforcer.

She swerved around to head in the other direction. Another enforcer already blocked the way. She veered down a side aisle. The heavy footfalls of the enforcers sounded behind her.

She turned again, nearly laying the bike over. It wouldn't help her, though. Chances of outrunning cyborg enforcers, even on a fast bike like hers, were slim to none. She would have to lose them.

A glance over her shoulder revealed no enforcers directly behind her, but their shouts and pounding feet echoed all around. She swerved the bike into an empty charging stall and left it there, hurrying among the parked cars, tugging on doors and praying someone had neglected to lock their vehicle. The sound of the enforcers came closer.

She sagged with relief when one of the cars popped open at her touch. She jumped into the backseat of the unlocked car and gagged. Empty fast-food bags, cups, and other wrappers littered the floor. Some still held half-eaten food. Whoever owned the car must be using filth as a theft deterrent. Too late to find somewhere else, though. The pounding of the enforcers was right on top of her.

Holding her breath, she locked the doors and flattened herself on the floor of the back seat, wriggling underneath the garbage as much as possible in the hopes no one peering in the windows would notice her. She pulled her hood up over her purple-streaked hair.

The enforcers bellowed her name, yanked on car doors, rapped on windows. A beam of light pierced through the windows above her. Pressley stopped breathing.

After a second, the light swung away, but she didn't move. Not even when the noise of the enforcers' searching receded into other areas of the parking garage. It was too easy to imagine one of them standing silently nearby, waiting for her to emerge. She kept a hand over her nose to try and keep out the smell of stale grease and waited for the end of the workday, still two hours away. Her legs grew cramped, and the nausea was relentless. At one point, when she could fight it no longer, she retched into a paper sack with a couple of moldy fries at the bottom, so loudly she thought for sure an enforcer would rip open the door and haul her away. But nothing happened. She curled up more tightly and tried to breathe through her mouth.

When she heard the sounds of people trickling in and cars and bikes pulling out, she sat up, brushed away the refuse, and clambered over the front seat. She'd have to act fast before the slob returned to their car. She opened the user interface panel and with a little finagling, got into the car's system. From there, it was pretty simple to find the ID of a neighboring car and convince this car it was that one instead. A minute later, when the other car started up, hers did too.

"I apologize for stealing your car," she announced to the empty seat beside her. "But it's a matter of life and death." She pulled her hood farther over her face as the car backed itself into the flow of traffic leaving Span Corp tower.

"Heading home," the car announced.

That wouldn't do. The car's owner would show up there eventually. She certainly couldn't go to her place either. There'd be enforcers there already.

Where to then? Was anywhere safe?

Bobby's place, maybe. Their relationship was hardly public knowledge. She hadn't even told Twiggy about it. She entered a random address a few blocks away from there. She could ditch the car and walk to Bobby's without leaving a trail.

"I'll leave the car where you can find it," she told the absent owner. "But you really should lock the doors. And clean this thing up. Gross!"

15

No one stopped her as she left the parking garage, so the enforcers weren't searching every vehicle. That was a blessing.

The car pulled into a parking spot half a block from the address she'd entered. She tumbled out, sucking in a breath of the fresh air—well, fresher than the car, anyway.

The slob had probably already reported his car missing, and it wouldn't take long to track it down. She zipped her jacket up to her chin and kept the hood low over her face in case the enforcers were using facial recognition drones to search for her.

Los Angeles rose around her in soaring canyons of neon and steel. Cars and bikes zipped by in the street beside her, sometimes honking and swerving around each other. People chatted and shouted on the sidewalks. Somewhere nearby, someone was busking on an electric guitar, and siren wails swelled and dimmed around it all.

A heaviness hung in the air beyond the heat and smog. Shoulders slumped with weariness. Faces pinched in hunger and despair. E-junkies sat on benches or slumped on sidewalks, eyes hidden behind tech glasses, bodies quivering. Many of these people had nowhere to go. Too many would be snatched up and exploited in the worst possible ways.

Pressley quickened her steps. She'd be among them now. Without Span Corp, she had no home, no access to healthcare, no damn rights at all. And even without enforcers after her, she wouldn't have been able to find something else. Not if Span Corp decided to black-ball her. She closed a fist around the data siphon in her pocket.

Halfway to Bobby's, she had to sit and rest on a bus bench next to a man who smelled like he hadn't washed in a decade. She scooted away from him, her arm wrapping around her belly.

"Got any cash for a war veteran, ma'am?" his voice rasped like an old window warped in its frame.

"No, sorry." As she stood, he grasped the hem of her jacket, but not with a hand. A metal pincer protruded from his wrist. Infection oozed from the joint. "Let go of me!" She yanked her jacket free and stumbled away, gagging. She'd never seen a prosthetic like that before. The kind of thing you might get if you couldn't see a real doctor. That was the kind of man who might opt to become an enforcer.

She hurried away and didn't stop until she reached Bobby's place above the vintage clothing store on east Eleventh. He wasn't home, but he'd keyed the door to her handprint. That said something about their relationship, she supposed, though she wasn't sure exactly what.

A narrow flight of stairs led up to the one-room loft. Pressley dropped to her knees in the little bathroom off the main living area and emptied her stomach into the toilet. She hadn't eaten all day, but that didn't stop her body from heaving just the same. When at last it stopped, she stripped off her garbage-tainted clothes and took a shower. She found a Lakers t-shirt and a pair of sweats that fit her okay in Bobby's drawers and collapsed onto the bed tucked into a nook in the far wall, more tired than she had any right to be.

If she'd had her phone, she might have tried calling him, but she didn't have it. Remaining alert would have been wise, but she was out before she could even think of a place to hide the data siphon.

She woke to Bobby Wilds kissing her on the cheek, rather than to an enforcer breaking down the door. Infinitely preferable.

"This is a nice surprise," he said when she stirred. He kissed her mouth, sinking onto the bed with his arms around her. That very nearly distracted her completely, but she pulled away and sat up.

"Bobby—"

"Hmm?" He tried to pull her down again.

"No, listen…" She intended to tell him about getting caught and fleeing the cyborg enforcers, but what came out was "I'm pregnant." Something she hadn't dared tell him in the two weeks since she'd found out.

Bobby sat up. "Really? You sure?"

"Positive. Just like the pregnancy test." She sighed. "I'm eight weeks now."

"And…it's mine?"

She gave him a withering glare.

"Right, no. I mean, of course, it's mine." He leaned back on his elbows and regarded her for a minute. He had a mop of unruly golden hair sticking out in every direction thanks to the Uber courier's helmet he wore making deliveries in the city all day. He still had on his gray courier's uniform, with a couple of buttons open on the top. They'd been dating about four months now, ever since she met him as her contact with Hazard Snow's campaign. Her sweet, sexy surfer boy.

"I thought Span Corp didn't allow—"

"They don't." She flopped back on the bed and covered her eyes with her elbow. "But I don't work for Span Corp anymore." Heaviness settled on her chest.

Bobby let out a whistle. "What happened?"

"They noticed my hacking."

She slipped out of bed and fetched the data siphon from the pile of clothes in the bathroom. "Here." She tossed it to Bobby. "Ransom McCleary sent his cyborg enforcers after me, so there must be something important in there. I haven't looked."

She hadn't actually seen any of the data she'd stolen from Span Corp, but that didn't mean Ransom McCleary wouldn't make her pay for it.

"How did you get away from the enforcers?"

"Stole a car that smelled like a McDonald's dumpster." She wrinkled her nose. "So disgusting." She quickly summed up the story for him.

"I'm impressed," Bobby said.

"Yeah? Well, you should be." Pressley found herself grinning in spite of herself. It was pretty impressive. "Can you contact Gil? Will Hazard protect me from the enforcers? Get me another job?"

Bobby winced. "I don't think it works like that. You get caught, you're on your own."

"Yeah, I figured." She sank into the little loveseat beneath the circular window that looked out over the city, blazing in the sunset glow. "I need food."

"Okay. I mean, I could order something in. What do you want?"

Pressley closed her eyes. "Pecan pie." She sighed, suddenly overwhelmed with desire for it. "With a mountain of whipped cream."

"Are you serious?"

"Anything else will make me puke."

"Really?"

"Really." She puckered up her face and pressed her hand to her belly. "And some ginger ale."

"You're kidding."

"No," she snapped. "It's the least you can do for me." She burst into tears, quite outside her own control. She wiped her face with the bottom of Bobby's Lakers t-shirt. "Oh my gosh. Twiggy." She'd almost forgotten. "Bobby, you have to contact my little sister. We were supposed to meet up for dinner. She'll be panicking when I don't show up." Pressley felt a little panicked herself. If anything bad happened to Twiggy because of her— "She's a worrier, and when she worries, she might do something stupid." Though *might* was probably a bit hopeful. Twiggy was sadly prone to doing stupid things. Like getting a holo-tat on a whim or dating losers pretending to be directors.

"Okay." He pulled out his phone.

"No. Don't call her. Span Corp could be monitoring her phone."

His eyes widened. "What about my phone?"

"Our relationship isn't public knowledge, but if they got a hold of my phone records before my kill order got rid of them..." She shrugged. "Best to assume they are."

"That isn't legal."

"Yeah, but neither is hacking into their system."

"Fair enough."

"You'll have to talk to her in person."

"You could write her a note that I can deliver." Bobby chuckled. "Like school kids a hundred years ago."

It wasn't a bad idea. "You could Uber her some food with a note inside the bag. You have paper and pen?"

"Yep. It's actually remarkably useful in my line of work." He rummaged around a drawer in the kitchen and emerged with a spiral-bound memo book and a gel pen. "You know how to use these, right?"

Pressley rolled her eyes. "They do still teach it in school, you know." But she felt a little awkward at it, truth be told, trying to keep her letters legible.

Dear Twiggy,

I am safe, so please don't worry. Don't say anything to Span Corp. They are wrong about me. I'll straighten it all out and see you soon.

All my love,
Press

Ugh. It felt like a lie. She ripped the note out of the memo book anyway, folded it in half, and handed it to Bobby. "She'll be at my place or her dorm." If she wasn't at a party or something.

"I'll deliver this and get you some pie." He kissed her cheek. A surge of affection stirred up more tears in the corners of her eyes.

"Thanks, babe. Be careful."

"Don't answer the door." Bobby retrieved his phone and left.

"Yeah, thanks, Mom," Pressley muttered. She paced the length of the loft—ten steps each direction—until she realized anyone in the shop below would be able to hear her. Particularly if that anyone was an enhanced cyborg.

She leaped onto the bed and pulled her knees up to her chest, listening for the sound of her death coming for her. Her eyes lit on the data siphon sitting on the little kitchen table. All these months she'd never once looked through what she'd stolen from Span Corp. She'd turned the siphons over to Bobby, who got them to Gil via dead drops. That was the way Hazard Snow wanted it. The less Pressley knew, the better. Hell, she'd never even met the man—just seen him at campaign rallies or on TV. But if she'd found something really juicy before she got caught, she might use it to convince Hazard to help her. If he really believed in all the stuff he spouted about fairness, equity, justice, and prosperity for all, then he wouldn't just leave her on the streets, would he? She sure hoped not. His idealism was the reason she'd gotten involved in the first place.

She slipped off the bed and tiptoed the few steps to the table. The tabletop computer activated at her touch, and the display popped up in front of her. She turned on the data siphon and connected to Bobby's home system.

Soon she had a list of dozens of deleted emails, texts, and other files. Ooh. She leaned forward. This was Ransom McCleary's personal data, not just company files. She'd dug deep indeed. No wonder she'd caught unwanted attention.

She found correspondence with big-shots all over the world—celebrities, politicians, even the president. There were video files, too, and she was fairly certain she didn't want to watch, but one of them was marked *extreme*, meaning it definitely contained incriminating content. She'd have to at least check it out. She sucked in her breath.

What she saw wasn't exactly the salacious sex tape she'd feared, though maybe that's what Ransom McCleary had intended to make. A young, pretty Asian girl sat on the edge of a gigantic bed in an opulent bedroom. She wore a skimpy silk negligee and a defiant expression. She couldn't have been any older than Twiggy.

Ransom McCleary stepped out from behind the camera and moved toward the girl. The head of Span Corp, and the richest man in the world, was in his sixties, tall and broad, with a hard face covered in dark scruff and a bald head. Pressley grimaced at the sight of him.

Everything in his bearing spoke of a man used to being obeyed, but the girl on the bed shouted something at him as he approached. The video had no sound, so Pressley didn't know what she said. The girl glared at McCleary, and he backhanded her so hard she fell off the bed.

Pressley gasped.

The girl scrambled to her feet. Blood dribbled from her nose, yet she continued to scream at McCleary, her delicate hands balled into fists.

McCleary smashed his own fist, twice as large as the girl's, into her already bloody face. She crumpled, but McCleary didn't stop. He pummeled the poor girl in a savage rage. Pressley covered her mouth with her hand, bile rising. The girl curled into a ball, but it did no good. McCleary stood and kicked her over and over. Blood pooled around her. He didn't stop until she was far beyond ever talking back to him again.

Pressley's hand trembled against her mouth. She slid off the kitchen stool and stumbled into the bathroom for another round of retching. If only she could purge from her brain the brutality she'd witnessed. Ransom McCleary's hard face. And the girl. Oh, that poor girl.

Pressley squeezed her eyes shut and leaned her forehead against the toilet seat, but it didn't help. Her heart wouldn't stop its wild racing.

That poor girl. Bleeding and broken. Lifeless.

The door to the loft thumped open. Pressley scrambled to her feet. She slammed the bathroom door and braced herself against it, though she doubted that would stop an enforcer.

A moment later, a gentle knock sounded. "Press?" Bobby whispered.

She pulled the door open. "He killed a girl."

Bobby's eyes widened. "Who did?"

"Ransom McCleary." Her voice rose. "He beat her to death. It was awful." She wrapped her arms around his waist, and he held her, stroking her hair until she stopped trembling.

"How do you know?"

"There's a vid. On the data siphon. I watched it." She shuddered. "This is everything Hazard Snow has been after."

Pressley spotted a take-out bag and disposable cup on the table.

"Your pie and ginger ale," Bobby said.

"Thanks, but I don't think I can eat." The soda might help, though. She took a tentative sip, cold and soothing. "Is Twiggy okay? You gave her the note?"

His forehead creased. "She's gone."

"Damn. Did you check her dorm? Talk to her roommate?" She took another sip of ginger ale.

"Pressley."

The tone of his voice stopped her cold. "What?"

"I found this at your place." He handed her an iridescent message wafer. She ran her thumb across it, and an image appeared on the surface. Pressley gasped. It was Twiggy in her hot-pink pigtails, looking even younger than usual with wide, frightened eyes.

"Ms. Amelia Pierce has been detained by Span Corp and will remain in custody until Ms. Pressley Pierce has been located and remanded to Span Corp. Please contact Span Corp within forty-eight hours with any information regarding Pressley Pierce. Thank you."

Bobby grabbed her by the shoulders as she lunged for the stairs. "You are not turning yourself in. They'll kill you."

"They took Twiggy." She slumped, defeated, against his chest. "What if they kill her?"

"Even Span Corp couldn't justify executing an innocent college girl."

"You don't know what Span Corp is capable of. Ransom McCleary is pure evil. You didn't see what I did."

Her stomach roiled again, and she buried her face in Bobby's chest. It wouldn't matter if she turned herself in. If she gave up the data siphon. They'd kill her and Twiggy both to stop them from talking, no matter what they did or didn't know.

And Ransom McCleary would continue to savagely beat girls to death with complete impunity and glut himself on the labor of others.

Pressley carried the soda over to the window and cleared the glass with a touch. Sunset crept across the sky, and lights flickered on over the city. Someone's cranked-up bass thrummed past under the window. Skyscrapers rose glittering in the distance, and over them all Span Corp Tower cast a garish glow. She had to assume Twiggy was there somewhere, probably scared to death.

Ransom McCleary had a chokehold on this city Hell, on the entire country, for that matter. The tendrils of his influence stretched around the world. He could manipulate people and politics to suit his desires whenever he wanted. Given time he'd crush them all. With a touch and a sigh, she blacked the window glass.

"I have to rescue Twiggy and bring down Ransom McCleary for good."

"Maybe." Bobby took her hands. "But first we have to get you somewhere safe. You won't be able to avoid the enforcers much longer."

"How can I run and hide with my baby sister in danger?" she protested.

"Press, you have to think about your baby too."

"My…" What were those stupid tears doing in her eyes again?

"Our baby," Bobby said, "I mean, assuming you want the baby."

Oh, hell. She hadn't expected him to care about the baby. "I—" Her heart crowded into her throat. "I can't—"

He wilted a little, his hands going limp in hers.

"I can't think about that right now."

Bobby's hands tightened again, almost reflexively.

"Okay. We can find somewhere safe for you to hide." He reached into his pocket. "I ditched my phone and got these." He produced two pre-paid anonymous burner phones in little plastic packets. "So we can still keep in touch."

She took one from him and ripped it open. It wasn't a Span Corp phone, so, yeah, they might be able to use it. It wouldn't get great service everywhere, but it might work.

"Good thinking." She might have thought of it herself if she wasn't so scattered. It surprised her a little that Bobby had. She'd never thought of him as particularly intelligent. But maybe she was wrong.

"I'll get the data siphon to Gil and tell him what happened. Maybe he can convince Hazard to help."

"No." Pressley took a step back, finding her voice again. "No. I'm keeping the data siphon. You contact Gil. He won't answer a burner number, but you can text him. Or use a dead drop. Whatever. Tell him I found everything Hazard Snow is after. If he wants it, I'll give it to him when my sister is free."

Bobby pushed his hands through his hair. "Okay, I'll try. But we'd better get you out of the city. I don't know of anywhere you can go. Maybe we could scrounge up some camping equipment, or…"

"No."

"You can't be too picky here, bae."

"I don't need to camp," she said with a sigh. "I have a place to go. Out of the city. Off the grid. It'll be perfect." Unfortunately.

"Where's that?"

She sighed again. "Home."

II.

That decided, all that remained was getting her safely out of the city, or even safely out of Bobby's loft for that matter. She had to do something about facial recognition drones, and since she couldn't change her bone structure, she'd have to change what they thought they were looking for. And she'd have to purge any record of her past and Twiggy's. Anything that might connect her to the isolated homestead near Sacramento where she'd grown up. The place she'd sworn she'd never return to.

Bobby prevailed upon her to eat the pie while she used his computer to log into one of the many dummy accounts she'd created at Span Corp. That worked, and she was pleased to find they hadn't discovered all her backdoors into the system. She dug deeply to find the code beneath her facial recognition profile.

It was tedious work. She was surprised to find the pecan pie tasted even more delicious than she'd hoped. Unfortunately, the smell of Bobby's Chinese takeout mingled unpleasantly with the pie, leaving her tummy still unsettled. The ginger ale helped a little.

Her mind churned harder than her stomach. If she concentrated on the hacking, she could almost put aside the horrifying images of the murder Ransom McCleary had committed. Harder was setting aside her worry over Twiggy. She could have kicked herself into the next county for putting her kid sister in danger. Into the clutches of McCleary. The thought made her hands tremble so badly she could hardly code.

Twiggy had come to L.A. to find Pressley when she was only sixteen and had had enough of their mother's iron-fisted rules and isolated lifestyle. Pressley had done the same when she was eighteen and Twiggy just twelve. She had never expected her little sister to show up on her doorstep, bedraggled and determined, having hitchhiked her way there. And against the odds, Twiggy had finished high school remotely and gotten herself into college, just as Pressley had. And even if Twiggy was prone to normal freshman stupidity like parties and tattoos, Pressley was fiercely proud of her. The thought of McCleary or his enforcer goons hurting her because of something Pressley did? No.

She brought her fist down on the table and startled Bobby awake in his bed, where he'd fallen asleep.

"You okay?" Bobby asked.

She had no answer. As if any of this were okay. That was the other thing intruding on her thoughts. The look in Bobby's eyes when he said *our baby.* She had expected him to cut and run. But here he was buying her pecan pie and tossing his phone and giving up his bike and possibly his livelihood so she (and their baby) would be safe. She wasn't sure what to make of that. Or where this was heading. Or where she wanted it to be heading. Or if it could be heading anywhere with McCleary and his enforcers after her.

"Bae?"

She stood up. "I'm finished." It was after 4:00 in the morning.

"They won't recognize you?"

She shrugged. "If they have to use facial recognition drones, they won't. If they see me up close, well—I'm pretty sure they know what I look like."

"You need a disguise."

"I need something, yeah."

Bobby had a Dodgers beanie that Pressley pulled down over her purple streaks. She put on one of Bobby's courier uniform jackets over the top of the T-shirt and sweats and added a pair of sunglasses. Not a perfect disguise by any means, but with her profile tampering and a little stealth, it would do. She hoped, anyway.

Bobby beckoned her over to the closet that took up most of one wall. He pushed aside a pile of dirty clothes and pulled open the little trap door underneath, barely wide enough for a single person to fit through. A wooden ladder attached to the wall led down to a storage closet in the boutique below. The ladder looked to have been installed sometime in the last century and not used since. A thick layer of dust coated the rungs.

"Here. I used all my tips to get a cash card. So you can buy what you need. Be careful." Bobby enfolded Pressley in his arms, returning the lump to her throat. "Call me as soon as you get there."

That would be risky. If the enforcers took Bobby they'd find his burner.

"It's better if you call me," she said. "As soon as you're in touch with Gil."

If he could get in touch with Gil. If the only option was a message disk in a dead drop location, it could take days before they got a response. And who knew how many days Twiggy had. "Do whatever you have to do to get in touch with him."

"I will." Bobby pulled her tight against him. "I love you, Pressley. I mean that."

Pressley didn't know what to say to that. She wasn't sure she believed it. So, she just squeezed him hard and didn't say anything. He kissed the top of her head and let her go.

"Thanks, Bobby," she whispered. "For everything."

Dust stirred around her feet as she descended the ladder. Cobwebs danced against her cheeks. She sneezed and froze, listening for the closet below to open. When it didn't, she started cautiously down again. The boutique wouldn't be open this early in the morning, but you never knew when an enterprising shopkeeper might turn up to get ready for business, especially in this economy.

At last, she reached the bottom of the ladder and dropped a couple of feet to the closet floor. Empty boxes surrounded her in piles that stretched higher than she was tall. Looked like the closet mainly served as a reserve supply of cardboard.

Pressley swam through the boxes in an awkward dance, making an unholy amount of noise. Finally, she found the door with its old-fashioned knob. Locked. She jiggled it a few times, but it wouldn't turn. Why in the world would anyone lock up a bunch of empty boxes? Probably because it led to the upstairs apartment. Okay, maybe it made sense. But for a panicky moment she had no idea how she'd get out. Not like she could hack a doorknob. Then her fingers found the little button in the middle. She pressed it in, and it popped right out. The knob turned smooth as butter, and she spilled out into the back room of the boutique, dark and silent. Phew. She closed the closet door behind her, kicking a few boxes back inside before she did.

The place was empty, thank heavens, and she didn't think she'd tripped any alarms. Great thing about shop alarms is they were designed to keep people from getting in from the outside, not prevent them from leaving once they were inside. She paused for a minute by the front door, scanning the street outside for enforcers. At this hour, it was mostly deserted. She spotted a couple of vagrants lounging against the walls of the high rise across the street. A car went by, and someone on a bike.

Pressley stepped up to the door, which opened automatically at her approach, and out onto the sidewalk with the air of someone who belonged there, not someone who was sneaking away. She fought the urge to duck her head, instead glancing around casually, as if she were any innocent person stepping out of a closed boutique at 4:30 in the morning.

Bobby's bike waited in a charging stall right in front of the boutique. Pressley lowered the shades over her eyes and climbed on. No one tried to stop her. She pulled out and drove away before anyone could.

In the predawn light, Los Angeles glowed with a quiet shimmer, awaiting the rush of the day to come.

Pressley merged onto the freeway heading north up the coast.

Span Corp tower rose to her right, a neon ziggurat piercing the heavens, gleaming in the dimness, dominating the skyline just like Span Corp dominated all the other companies in the world. Dominated all their lives. *No more,* she vowed. Twiggy was in that vast tower somewhere.

"I'll get you out, sis. I promise." She lowered her head, hit the throttle, and sped away.

o o o

Six and half hours later, with nothing but a shopping bag with a few clothes and essentials she'd picked up at a Walmart somewhere, she turned off the main road and up the quiet country lane that led to the isolated little homestead she hadn't seen in eight years. Home.

It was like being on a different planet from the pulsing, glowing heart of L.A. A couple of chickens pecked in the grass under the shade of the venerable old apple tree. The two-story farmhouse that had stood here for over a century looked freshly painted but otherwise unchanged. When she stepped up onto the porch, a fat, marmalade cat on a weather-beaten rocker stretched and jumped off the chair.

"Duke?" Pressley reached out to pet him. "You're still around?"

The cat dodged her hand and stalked off the porch with his tail flipping in annoyance. Good old Duke.

Pressley hesitated at the door. It probably wasn't locked, but just walking in didn't feel right. She swallowed the lump in her throat, ignored the rising nausea, and knocked. After a few seconds, she almost turned and left. No one home. Oh, well. Maybe facing enforcers was preferable to facing Mom after all.

The door swung open, but it wasn't her mother standing there. It was a handsome man with graying hair and a neatly trimmed salt-and-pepper beard. "Hey."

"Oh." Pressley took a step back. She had not considered the possibility that her mother had moved away. Not with Duke still sitting on the porch. For a couple of seconds, her confused, exhausted brain refused to form words. She stood there with her mouth hanging open and panic forming in her chest.

The man regarded her calmly. "You're Pressley, right?"

Oh, no. The enforcers had already been here. She took another step back and grabbed the railing to keep herself from falling down the stairs.

The man held out his hand to shake. "I'm glad to meet you. My name is Malcolm Burke. I married your mother last year."

"Oh" was all she could get out. Again. Married her mother?

"I'm sorry I startled you." His hand was still extended.

Pressley's brain finally snapped to attention. She shook his hand. "I—yes, I'm Pressley. It's—good to meet you too."

He laughed with a warmth that seeped into her chest and made her feel a little strange.

"This must be quite a shock," Malcolm said. "Please come in. I'll get your mom."

Pressley followed him inside. The old, sagging sofa she remembered had been replaced with a new sectional in what looked like leather. The fireplace mantle held pictures of her and Twiggy, both years out of date, and a more recent wedding picture of her mom and Malcolm Burke in front of a building that looked like a fancy castle. She thought it was a temple for the church her mom had joined years ago. On the wall hung a display box full of medals like a soldier or a cop might receive.

She didn't have time to study it closely. A door opened down the hall and her mother flew into the living room, flinging her arms around Pressley and squeezing her tight enough to crack a rib. "You came home."

"Mom." Pressley wrapped stiff arms awkwardly around her mother. It wasn't the reception Pressley had expected, not a tirade about her purple hair and poor life choices. She offered her mom a tentative pat on the back.

At last, her mother stepped back and held her at arm's length. "I've been praying God would bring you back to me."

Pressley let out a laugh more like a sob. It sure wasn't God who'd brought her here.

"You and Twiggy both." Mom's eyes darted over Pressley's shoulder, full of such painful hope it cracked Pressley's heart.

"She's not here."

Mother blinked and focused back on Pressley. "That's okay. Someday, right? You know where she is? Is she okay?"

Pressley's breath rushed out of her. How was she supposed to answer that? "Uh, yeah. Yeah, she's in L.A. with me. Going to UCLA." She nodded lamely. "You'd be proud." Except for the holo-tat. Her chest hurt.

"Oh, I am," Mother said. "Proud of you both. Come sit down. You must be tired. Are you hungry?"

Hungry was putting it mildly. She was exhausted and starving and bordering on puking again. She nodded numbly and allowed Mom to lead her into the kitchen. The sturdy, old oak table had not been replaced. Mom ushered her into the seat that had once been her usual spot. Pressley had carved a heart into the tabletop with a pocketknife when she was twelve. Mom had grounded her for a week after that, but the heart remained. Pressley traced it with her finger.

"Let me get you both some lunch," Malcolm said. "I'm sure you two have a lot to talk about."

The less talking the better, Pressley thought. But her mom was already pulling up a chair beside her and squeezing her arm and smiling like there had never been any tension between them. Like all the fights and the tears and rifts had never happened. It made Pressley a little dizzy.

"Press," Mom said. "I have some wonderful news."

"You're married. I heard. That was quite a surprise."

"I would have given anything for you and Twiggy to be here for that." Mom smiled. "But that's not what

I meant." She cast a fond glance toward her husband. "I'm pregnant. You're going to have another sister or brother. I've been dying to tell you. I'm so glad you're here."

Pressley blinked, dumbfounded. "Wow, that's weird."

"Not really." Mom laughed. "I'm only forty-five, after all. You forget how young I was when you were born."

"No, I know." Pressley fiddled with the heart on the table. "That's not the weird part."

"Then what—" Mom gasped. "You're pregnant too."

"Yeah, I am." Her hands went unconsciously to her belly. Her jaw tightened.

Her mother clapped her hands. "This is fantastic."

And that really wasn't the reaction Pressley had expected. "No, it really is kind of weird."

"Maybe a little." Mom laughed again. "I'm thrilled. I'm going to be a grandmother."

Pressley leaned back in her chair and closed her eyes. Mom wasn't going to be thrilled when she learned about Twiggy and Ransom McCleary and Span Corp enforcers.

But she didn't need to know. As soon as Bobby contacted her again, Pressley could go back to L.A., hand over the data siphon, and bring Twiggy back here with her for a few days. If she could convince Twiggy this version of their mother was real. She wasn't sure she believed it herself.

"Tell me about the city," Mom said.

Malcolm spoke from the counter. "I'll make you two some sandwiches." No doubt on homemade, whole-grain bread with all organic ingredients. The food was better here, at any rate.

"Tell me everything." Mom's voice held a hint of the *I-gave-you-an-order* tone. Pressley cringed. Everything was not a good idea. She offered the sanitized version instead.

"I graduated from UCLA with a degree in computer science, and I got a job at Span Corp."

Mother winced, opened her mouth, and shut it again.

"Yeah, it's every bit as bad as you think." She shrugged. "But it gives me a place to live and food on the table."

Mother gave her an appraising look. "Are you happy there?"

She hesitated. "At Span Corp? Not really. And I guess the city isn't as glamorous as I thought it would be. There are a lot of problems. But there are a lot of good things too. I love the fast pace, the diversity, the excitement. The beach." She smiled. Really, there was a lot of good if you knew where to look, and she had just wanted to make it better. For herself, for Twiggy, for everyone.

Mom nodded, her forehead creased. "And what about Twiggy? Is she going into computer science too?"

"No. Twiggy wants to be an actress."

"An actress? Wow. I never knew that about her."

As if Mom had ever asked what they wanted to do with their lives. Ever consulted them about their opinion on anything.

"I'm so proud of you." Mom took Pressley's hands. Tears glistened in her eyes again. "Ever since you left, and then Twiggy too, I've thought about all the things I should have done differently." She shook her head. "I hope we can start over fresh."

Pressley's throat tightened. This pregnancy hormone crap was no joke. That would also explain this new person who had appeared in place of Annelise Pierce. Pressley nodded wordlessly, patted her mother's hand, cleared her throat, and tried to speak.

"I made my share of mistakes too." Some she couldn't very well tell her mother. Maybe she shouldn't have come. A strange mix of gratitude and regret percolated in her belly.

"Nobody's perfect," Mom said. "Let's make a promise to just move forward from here, right?"

"All right." It might not be possible, but maybe it was worth a shot.

∘ ∘ ∘

Later that night, alone in her old bedroom on the second floor, Pressley held the burner on her palm and willed Bobby to call her. The phone remained silent, unused. She reminded herself that there hadn't been enough time to get in touch with Hazard, much less free Twiggy, but surely he could tell her something, couldn't he? Really, she just wanted to hear his voice. To see if he still had that look in his eyes from when he told her he loved her, or if having a day to think things over had changed his mind. Calling him seemed too risky, though she really hoped he hadn't been picked up by the enforcers.

Pressley curled up on her old bed. The burner went onto the nightstand with the peppermint tea and toast her mom had made her. They reminded her of Corny's Coke and crackers. She hoped the enforcers had left him alone.

I shouldn't have come. I should have turned myself in, baby or not.

A quiet knock sounded at her door. She sat up. The movement left her a bit dizzy. "Come in."

She expected to see her mother checking in on her again, but it was Malcolm who opened the door.

"Sorry to bother you. I saw the light on and wondered if we might have a little chat."

"I'm pretty worn out."

"It won't take long." He smiled, but it did little to soften the seriousness of his expression. He motioned with his head toward the stairs like he expected her to follow.

Pressley rose warily. He'd been kind and friendly towards her all day, but now she felt like a teenager being called on the carpet by the father she'd never had.

Malcolm gestured her onto the couch and sat across from her on a wooden rocker. "I'm glad you're here. I've never seen your mom happier. She has wanted you and your sister back in her life for a long time."

"I wish Twiggy were here," Pressley said. "Maybe next time."

"Yes." Malcolm leaned forward with his elbows on his knees and clasped his hands. His arms held a strength that belied his age. His gray-blue eyes met hers, probing and intense. "But I couldn't help but notice you came here without any bags, only a few things I think you bought on the way."

Pressley glanced at the tell-tale creases in the pajama pants she'd just taken out of the package. She looked back at Malcolm, tight-lipped.

"Seems to me, if you needed some place to hide in today's world, this would be an excellent spot."

"It would, yes."

Malcolm raised an eyebrow and waited for her to say more. Pressley had no intention of obliging.

"What kind of trouble are you in?" he asked when the silence between them stretched too thin. "Does it have something to do with the father of your baby? Did he hurt you or threaten you?"

"Bobby? No." She shook her head for emphasis. "He's a decent guy. He wouldn't do anything like that."

"But you are on the run from someone. That's obvious. Tell me what's going on. Maybe I can help you. At any rate, if danger is headed this way, I need to know what's coming."

She glanced at the case of medals hanging above the mantle. He looked dangerous himself just then, and perhaps he was, but what could he do against cyborg enforcers? She kept silent.

Malcolm's expression darkened. "Pressley, believe it or not, I do care about what happens to you. I'm not naïve, and I'm not blind to how the world works. I can help you if you'll trust me. I will do everything in my power to protect our family."

Our family? Did he mean that?

"That includes you and your sister and your unborn baby, and even your boyfriend if you want it to. But I will not allow you to carelessly endanger us. So, if you can't or won't tell me what's going on, you'll have to make some excuse for leaving first thing in the morning. Just please do me a favor and be as gentle with your mother as you can be. Don't break her heart again." He stood. "Goodnight."

"Malcolm," Pressley said, her decision made in an instant. "I'm running from Span Corp. From Ransom McCleary and his cyborg enforcers."

Malcolm's brow furrowed.

The story came out in a rush, all of it. Bobby, her undercover work for Hazard Snow, the murder video, and what happened to Twiggy.

"The enforcers took her to get to me," Pressley said. "I'm scared that—"

A door banged open down the hall. "Pressley, you lied to me?" Mom stormed into the front room in a nightgown and slippers, eyes snapping in anger. "Twiggy's in danger and you didn't mention it all day? You didn't come here to see me at all, did you? Of course, you didn't. I don't even know why I'm surprised. Why I thought—"

"Annelise." Malcolm took a conciliatory step toward her. She shot him an *I'll-deal-with-you-later* glare.

"Mom, I didn't mean…"

"What? You didn't mean what, Pressley? Didn't mean to let me think you'd changed? That things could be different between us?"

And there she was. The mother Pressley had been expecting from the start.

"You should have told me about Twiggy when you got here. I deserve to know!"

"I didn't want to worry you. I didn't think I would need to tell you anything."

"Are you kidding me?" Mother's eyes blazed.

"Annelise," Malcolm tried again. He put his arm around his wife's shoulders and led her down the hall, whispering earnestly into her ear. Mom shook her head fiercely, but Malcolm kept his arm tight around her and hustled them both into the bedroom to continue the hushed conversation in private.

Pressley folded her arms around herself and shivered. She considered running now, before they came back out, but where would she go? Mother's little farmstead was miles away from civilization, and she didn't have anywhere else to go. She had no money except what little remained on the cash card, no food, no identity. She thumped onto the couch and grabbed a throw pillow adorned with an embroidered rooster, as if the pillow could shield her somehow from the harsh reality. This was seventeen all over again, but worse because this time she'd endangered her sister's life. She hugged the pillow against her chest. Nausea built in her gut just thinking about Twiggy and her mother. Pressley clenched her jaw, but the sickness in her stomach intensified. She jumped to her feet, tripping over the furniture in her haste to get to the kitchen sink.

When the heaving stopped, she rinsed out her mouth and leaned heavily on the counter, gulping in breaths. Footsteps sounded behind her. She stiffened. "Don't worry. I'll be leaving as soon as I get my things together."

"No you won't," Malcolm said. "That would be suicide."

Pressley turned around. Malcolm still had his arm around Mom's shoulders. Mother's eyes were watery and red, but the anger had left her face. "I don't want to lose either of my girls."

"I don't want you to either. I'm sorry I didn't tell you. I thought I could spare you the worry."

"I would rather know the truth than be spared." Anger crept back into her voice. Malcolm tightened his hold on her shoulder.

Pressley sighed. "I love Twiggy as much as you do. I will get her back. I just need a safe haven for a few days until I make that happen." She explained her plan.

Mother shot Malcolm a worried look.

"That won't work," Malcolm said.

"Why not?" She bristled a little. Sure, the plan was desperate, but did Malcolm have a better idea?

"I know Hazard Snow. We served together in the war."

Ah. Maybe he did. If he knew Hazard Snow, then maybe… She took an eager step forward. "Can you contact him? Are you friends?"

"We were close for a while—until I came to know his true character during our time in Hong Kong. I'll spare you the details, but he is most definitely not a good man. He won't help you. He won't risk his own ambitions. He'll more likely try to take the siphon from you with thugs of his own."

"Damn." Pressley kicked the cabinet behind her. Mother looked ready to protest, but Malcolm staved it off.

"Why don't we all go sit down. We have a lot to discuss."

Pressley trailed after the two of them back into the front room. She grabbed the rooster pillow again, this time as a shield against the frustration rising inside her. She wanted to tell Malcolm he was wrong about Hazard Snow, but she couldn't.

"I started working for Hazard Snow in the first place because he talks so big about freedom and personal liberties," she said. "About breaking the hold of corrupt, greedy corporations like Span Corp."

"You're more like your mother than you think," Malcolm said, squeezing Mother's hand.

Pressley closed her eyes, shuddering. Nausea continued to roll in her gut. "Maybe so. I wanted more freedom when I left home, but I found even less. It's nearly impossible to live without working for some big corporation. Span Corp is the largest, but there are others too. Once they hire you, it's like they own you. You live where they say, and anything you create—from computer code to poetry to…anything—belongs to them. My friend Corny would love to write music, but he can't. And you can hardly make any decisions about your own life or health without their approval. I wouldn't be able to keep this baby if I stayed with Span Corp."

Her voice rose, warming to the topic she felt so passionate about but seldom got to express. "But if you quit, or worse, get fired, and Span Corp black-balls you—and they will—you'll never find a job anywhere else. And when you end up on the street—" She stopped. Mother had gone white. "I don't even want to think about it." Pressley closed her eyes and drew in a breath.

"Oh, Pressley. I had no idea," Mother whispered.

"And I just couldn't stand it, you know? I hated that I couldn't even choose where I wanted to live. I hated to think of Twiggy becoming as trapped as I felt with all her movie-star dreams scattered. I hated seeing the poverty and people suffering and not being able to do anything about it." She thought of the old veteran with a rusty metal claw for a hand.

"I mean, sure, there are perks to working at Span Corp. The medical center, the gyms, gaming lounges, snacks. But is all that really worth it?" She hugged the rooster. "I thought this was something I could do. I could help Hazard Snow get elected, even if it was by illegally digging up dirt on a powerful opponent. He needs what I found on the data siphon. Using it as leverage is the only way I can think of to get Twiggy back."

"Will McCleary hurt Twiggy?" Tears colored Mother's voice.

Pressley bit her lip. She couldn't say no, no matter how badly she wanted to. "I think—we'd better get to her as fast as we can." She tossed the pillow aside.

"I was counting on Hazard Snow to be able to change things. Maybe he's the only one who can."

"Maybe not the only one," Mom said. She looked fondly at Malcolm and patted his knee. He squeezed her hand. "Pressley, you have a good heart. I admire that," Mother said.

Pressley expected a "but" to come after that, but none did. Mom had never praised her like that before.

"Here's what I suggest," Malcolm said. "I'll come to L.A. with you. I'll talk to Hazard Snow. He'll listen to me."

Pressley sat up straighter. "You know how to get in touch with him? And he'll listen to you?"

"I can't call him directly, but if you tell him I want to see him, he won't say no."

"You have some dirt on him? From the war?"

"Let's just say we went through enough together to give him a reason to help your sister."

"Sounds good to me."

"You really think he'll help you?" Mom asked. "He won't try and get you out of the picture?"

"I saved his life," Malcolm said. "That should mean something to him."

"It's more pull than I have," Pressley said. "How soon can we leave?"

"First thing in the morning," Malcolm said. "We could all use some rest."

"But Twiggy…"

"Don't worry, Mom," Pressley said. "We'll get her back. I promise." She felt a little more confident with someone like Malcolm Burke on her side.

· · ·

The night passed quickly. When Pressley awoke the silent burner greeted her like an unspoken accusation. *Where are you, Bobby?* She picked up the phone and curled her fingers around it. Bobby had been so quick to help her, not even thinking of himself. She bit her lip. She was carrying his child, but what did she really want from him? She didn't want him to get hurt, she knew that much. Not physically or emotionally. She didn't know if she could prevent either one.

Malcolm rapped on her door. "We leave in thirty," he called through it. "Your mom has breakfast ready."

Of course she did. Cooking was how Mom handled stress. She was very good at it too. Pressley willed her stomach to behave itself, showered quickly, and hurried downstairs with the burner and the data siphon tucked safely into her bra.

Her tummy gurgled only slightly at the scent of scrambled eggs, ham, and toast. No coffee because her mom didn't drink it, but Pressley didn't mind. Her stomach didn't like the smell of coffee right now.

Mom piled up a plate for her and sat down across the table. Malcolm, it seemed, had already eaten and was outside making sure his truck was in working order. After only a couple of bites, Pressley's stomach rebelled again. She set down her fork.

"You need to eat," her mom admonished. "You're building another person."

"Then my body ought to stop tossing back everything I give it."

"It'll get better," Mom said. "Trust me." She patted Pressley's arm. "I haven't thrown up once this morning."

"I still think this is weird."

Mom chuckled. "Yeah, it is a little weird."

A gunshot fragmented the gentle, morning peace. Both women came out of their seats.

"Malcolm!" Mom lunged toward the front room.

"No!" Pressley grabbed her arm and threw them both to the floor as the windows shattered inward.

The back door splintered open. Pressley covered her mother with her own body, not daring to look up. She could hear the heavy tread of the enforcer coming toward them. More gunshots thundered through the house. Pressley flinched, waiting for the bullets to tear through her and her mother beneath her. Mother screamed.

Strong hands gripped Pressley's shoulders and lifted her up.

"You hurt?"

Malcolm.

Pressley shook her head. He gathered her mother up. "Are you all right?"

Mother moaned and buried herself in her husband's shoulder. He wrapped his arms tight around her.

Pressley looked over at the dead enforcer lying on the remains of the back door with a massive hole in his chest. A lot of his body was cybernetic, but a lot of it was flesh and blood, too. She looked away, gagging.

Malcolm handed Mother over to Pressley. "You two get to the truck. Quickly. I'll be right behind you."

Pressley hustled her mom outside. Both of them had cuts on their faces and bare arms from the broken windows. Pressley's hands shook so badly she almost couldn't get the truck door open. Just beyond the driveway, another dead enforcer lay in the dirt.

Malcolm had taken them both down singlehandedly in all of thirty seconds? "Where did you find this guy?" she asked her mom.

"At church." Her laughter was almost frantic.

Pressley hoisted her into the cab of Malcolm's pickup truck and climbed in beside her. They clasped hands. Pressley couldn't tell if she or Mom was trembling more.

"I don't know how they found me here," she whispered. "I'm so sorry."

"We're alive," Mom said. Her grip on Pressley's fingers tightened. "That's what matters."

Malcolm put both the enforcers' guns on the floor under their feet. "Be ready to grab those if we run into trouble."

"We can't—we can't just leave them," Mom stammered, looking at the dead man over her shoulder.

Malcolm started the truck. "I called the sheriff's office and told them we'd been attacked."

Pressley stiffened.

"I didn't mention you," Malcolm said. "And I'm not hanging around to wait for them. There could be more of these enforcers out there."

He pulled the truck out of the driveway and onto the empty country road that led away from the homestead.

"I'm so sorry," Pressley repeated. "I don't know how they found me. I wiped all my personal data."

"Who knew were you coming?"

"No one."

"What about your boyfriend?"

"I told him I was going home. I didn't tell him where." Pressley didn't want to believe that Bobby might have compromised her. Might have told someone she was going to her mother's and led the enforcers straight to the farmhouse. No, he wouldn't have done that. Not unless he was under some kind of duress.

She took a steadying breath. "Bobby gave me a blank cash card, and I used that to get the new clothes. They might have studied all the security cams between here and L.A., but I altered my facial recognition profile. They'd have to search pretty close to see me, and even that wouldn't tell them where I was headed."

"Twiggy knows," Mom said faintly. "She knows where we live."

And her sister could have been threatened or tricked into giving up that information. "That means she's still alive, right?" Pressley said.

"Oh, Lord," her mother sighed. She lowered her head and began to mutter what Pressley assumed was a prayer. They could certainly use all the help they could get.

III.

They arrived in L.A. under a sweltering sun. Span Corp tower filled their view as they drove into the city. "Is that where Twiggy is?" her mother asked.

"Probably. It's like its own little city."

Even in the harsh light of noonday, Span Corp Tower seemed to glow, the holo displays spilling over the sides. Tens of thousands of people worked there, blissfully unaware of the rot that lived at the core. Or content to ignore it. It cast a long shadow over the city.

When Pressley had volunteered for Hazard Snow's campaign, she'd expected to distribute flyers or help people register to vote. Instead, Gil Wang had contacted her and told her that Hazard could use her computer skills and connection to Span Corp for a different, less legal, more dangerous project, and she had jumped on it. She hadn't thought she'd get caught.

But, then, she hadn't thought she'd dig up anything as incriminating as what she'd seen.

But if Malcolm was to be believed, Hazard Snow didn't deserve her support any more that Span Corp and its CEO. It wasn't hard to believe, though. Hazard was seeking a position of power and doing whatever he could to secure it. Maybe no one could be trusted.

Malcolm checked them into a hotel that had to be at least a hundred years old, but it had the advantage of being in a run-down, forgotten neighborhood—a place largely left alone. So they'd put up with orange shag carpet and the strong smell of weed and beds that sagged precipitously in the middle.

Malcolm took the burner from her and called Bobby. Pressley held her breath. She and her mother sat together on one of the ratty beds, out of sight, just in case Bobby or his burner had been compromised.

"Press?" Bobby stopped short when he saw Malcolm's face. "Where is Pressley?" His voice took on an angry edge.

"She's safe," Malcolm said. "We need you to set up a meeting with Hazard Snow. You tell him Malcolm Burke wants to see him. He knows who I am."

"Well, I don't know who you are. And how am I supposed to know Pressley's actually safe? I want to talk to her."

"We're not going to risk that, kid. I want her safe just as much as you do. I'm her stepfather."

Pressley raised an eyebrow at that. They'd only met twenty-four hours ago. Her mother squeezed her hand and nodded as if in confirmation of his assertion.

"I know your name is Bobby Wilds, and I know Pressley is carrying your child."

"Hey—"

"I know her sister Twiggy is in danger."

"She's not the only one," Bobby muttered.

"Yes. That's why you're going to set up a meeting for me with Hazard Snow. Today."

For a long moment, Bobby didn't respond. "I can't just call him up, you know." He sounded like a bowstring stretched taut and ready to snap.

"I know. Hazard Snow won't help you."

"I tried to tell Press that, but—"

"But he will listen to me. He'll see me. You don't have to mention Pressley at all. Just tell him Malcolm Burke wants to see him. That's all you have to do."

"You're sure Pressley is safe?'

"I'm sure, and I'm going to keep her that way. Can we count on you?"

Bobby puffed out a breath. "I'll do my best, man."

"All we can ask." Malcolm ended the call and shot Pressley a questioning look. "Can we count on him?"

"I sure hope so."

Mom put her arm around Pressley. "He seemed sincere in his concern for you."

"Yeah." She closed her eyes with a sigh. "I sure hope so."

o   o   o

The jangle of the burner jarred Pressley awake. She hadn't thought it possible to sleep on the old bed, especially with the threat of enforcers ever-present, but apparently the sheer exhaustion of pregnancy could overcome many obstacles. She pushed herself up and watched Malcolm answer the phone. It wasn't a voice call—only text. An address and a time. 8:00 pm. A couple of hours from now.

"I'll go," Malcolm said. "You two can wait for me here."

"No," Mother jumped in before Pressley could raise her own protest. "If those enforcers find us again, we need you nearby."

"She's right," Pressley said. "We're better off sticking together."

Malcolm frowned. "Okay. We'll stick together. But let me take the lead here. I'll negotiate Hazard's help in freeing Twiggy in exchange for the data siphon."

"Then we all go home," Mom said. "At least until Ransom McCleary is behind bars."

63

Pressley held her tongue. She doubted very much Twiggy would agree to leave L.A. for any reason. And where did this plan leave Bobby? Would Mom welcome him at the farmstead? Would he even come? They'd have to cross that bridge when they came to it. She nodded her assent.

Two hours later, they pulled up in Malcolm's truck at the offered address, which turned out to be a swanky sushi bar. "Does he want to meet you for dinner?" Pressley whispered as they climbed out of the truck. Her newly bought tank and jeans seemed woefully out of place, and Malcolm and Mom both looked like the farmers they were.

Malcolm didn't seem bothered by it, though. He ushered them in the front doors and up to the maître d'. "We're here to see Hazard Snow."

The Japanese man, who wore a natty tux, looked down his nose at the three of them. His mouth tightened. He touched the screen on his podium. Green and blue lights chased around the edges and down the sides. His lips tightened further. "One moment, please." The man walked stiffly away, motioning to one of the servers to go and keep an eye on them.

"Bobby might have told us we needed to dress up," Pressley muttered. Not that she had anything dressy to wear anyway.

"Hazard's trying to get us flustered," Malcolm said. He met Pressley's eyes. "Don't let him."

The maître d' was back a minute later with Bobby Wilds in tow. Bobby wore an expensive-looking gray suit with a deep blue dress shirt underneath, unbuttoned at the collar. He was more nicely dressed than Pressley had seen him before. Although the suit fit him well, Bobby looked distinctly uncomfortable wearing it. When his eyes lighted on Pressley, a look of shock came over him, with relief close on its heels.

He pushed past the maître d' and wrapped his arms around her. She hugged him back, her heart pounding in sudden fear. What was he doing here?

"I don't think we can trust Hazard," he whispered in her ear.

"I know."

"Be careful. He doesn't know about us."

"Okay."

He let her go, letting his lips brush her cheek as he pulled away. Then he seemed to fall into some new persona, all business, but Pressley could see the anxiety underneath his slick veneer.

He held out his hand. "Malcolm Burke?"

"Bobby, right?" Malcolm shook his hand. "This is Annelise, my wife and Pressley's mother."

"Nice to meet you." Bobby shook Mom's hand. She nodded without speaking. He focused on Malcolm again. "I don't think Mr. Snow expected you to bring guests."

"I don't think we were informed this would be a dinner party."

"Right," Bobby muttered. "Follow me, please." He glanced at Pressley for half a second and motioned them forward. The maître d' moved back into position behind his podium. Pressley leaned over to Mom and Malcolm and whispered, "Don't mention me and Bobby."

Mom nodded. Bobby led them through the restaurant, filled with the clinking of dishes, murmur of conversation and laughter, and soft techno music. A bar of blue light ran around the top edge of the wall, and giant screens projected scenes of nature, bright fish flitting through crystal blue ponds, starscapes, acrobats, and dancers.

Somber-faced servers carried trays of gourmet sushi to the guests, and the chefs stood behind long counters preparing their masterpieces. Pressley had never been anywhere nearly so fancy. She tried to take Malcolm's advice to heart and not let it unsettle her. He walked ahead of her with all the confidence of a conquering general. Mom held his arm and moved like a queen. Pressley felt more like a vagrant, rumpled and smelly, and wanted to hide.

Bobby pushed back a sliding screen that partitioned off a private area for small gatherings. Hazard Snow waited there, seated at a round table wearing a cream-colored suit and a smug expression. He was a handsome man with dark hair and eyes and a fair complexion. Gil sat beside him with a smug, bejeweled grin on his rat-like face. Pressley wondered if the gems embedded in his teeth were real and how he could afford something like that. His suit matched Bobby's, making it look like some lackey uniform they both wore.

Hazard came to his feet as Bobby pulled the screen closed behind them. "Malcolm Burke!" Hazard held out his hands. "My old friend. How many years has it been now?"

"Not enough," Malcolm said as if it were a joke. The expression on his face said it wasn't, but Hazard laughed and stepped around the table to embrace Malcolm with plenty of back thumping.

"Please introduce me to these charming young ladies," Hazard oozed.

"My wife, Annelise." Hazard took Mom's hand and kissed it.

"And I believe you know her daughter, Pressley Pierce."

"I don't believe I've had the pleasure." He kissed Pressley's hand as well, his lips cold as ice against her skin.

"I work for your campaign." She slid her hand away from his. Had she really thought this man would make a difference in the world? "Though I only had contact with Gil here." She nodded at him.

"Yes, so I've heard. Please—" He gestured to the table. "Sit. I have dinner already ordered. I wasn't expecting these lovelies, but that's not a problem." He fluttered a hand toward a server hovering in the corner. The man nodded and left. A bulkier and more stony-faced man wearing an eyepiece over one eye lurked in another corner of the room. Pressley assumed he was a bodyguard, though if Hazard had half the fighting skills Malcolm did, he wouldn't need one.

The man scanned them with his eyepiece, trying to be subtle about it. Pressley hoped her altered facial recognition profile was giving him fits. It amused her to think so. She sat next to her mother. Hazard took a seat across from Malcolm. Bobby shuffled, as if he didn't know whether to stay or go, until Hazard motioned him brusquely into the seat beside him. Bobby slid into place and avoided looking directly at Pressley or anyone else for that matter.

"To what do I owe this pleasure, Malcolm? I assume you didn't come all the way to Los Angeles just to catch up on old times."

Malcolm folded his hands on the table. "I've come about my stepdaughter. Pressley's sister, Amelia, or

Twiggy, as they call her. She's been taken into custody by Span Corp."

"Kidnapped," Pressley said. "She was kidnapped by enforcers." She leaned forward, her hands spread on the table. "I found something on the latest data siphon. Something bad enough that McCleary noticed it. I barely got away from Span Corp Tower. He took my sister to get to me, but there's no way he'll let Twiggy go now, even if I turn myself in. If Ransom McCleary finds me, my sister and I are as good as dead.

The server reappeared with an assistant, each bearing an array of food on a large tray. Hazard Snow appraised Pressley over the table as they spread out the meal. No one made any move to touch the food. When the servers withdrew, Hazard leaned back in his chair. "I fail to see what any of that has to do with me."

"I've been siphoning data for you for months. What I found this time will put Ransom McCleary behind bars for the rest of his life. Isn't bringing down Span Corp what you're after?"

"My dear Ms. Pierce, I would never hire anyone to engage in illegal activity."

Pressley ground her teeth. So, that was how he wanted to play it? "I see. I wonder who Gil here has been delivering the data siphons to."

"I don't know what you're talking about." Gil flashed another glittering grin.

"So, Bobby's just been tossing them in the trash?" She folded her arms and glared at him.

Bobby lifted his head. "I just left them at dead drops." He stuffed a piece of sushi into his mouth and dropped his eyes again, the traitor.

"Mr. Snow," Mother said. "You have the resources to help my daughters. Please."

Hazard held up a hand to stop her. "If I helped every random e-junkie hacker who came begging to me, I'd be out on the streets myself."

Pressley had to physically bite her tongue to keep from responding to that.

Malcolm casually took a tray of sushi and slid a few pieces onto his plate. "You know, I was thinking about Hong Kong just the other day. What times we had there. You remember Hong Kong, my friend?"

"I try not to think about it." Hazard took a sip of wine, his face carefully bland, revealing nothing.

"Really? I think about it all the time." Malcolm fixed Hazard in a stony glare.

Mother waved off a server trying to pour wine in her glass. She laid her hand on Malcolm's arm. The two men stared each other down, sharing some secret memory between them. A memory that puckered Malcolm's brow and haunted Hazard's eyes.

"I'm sure some of your campaign backers would be interested to know about Hong Kong."

"Are you threatening me?" Hazard asked, his voice low. "My brother-in-arms? You know what it was like. You were there. Are you going to judge me for the things that happened there?" His hands curled into fists "Have you told your wife all about it? Do you want me to?"

Mother's hand tightened on Malcolm's arm. Bobby's eyes flitted between Hazard and Malcolm, occasionally lighting on Pressley. He looked like a fox caught in a trap, about to chew his own leg off to escape. Gil chuckled to himself and wolfed down his sushi.

"I'm just looking for some help for my family," Malcolm said in a voice quiet and deadly.

Hazard's bodyguard lowered his head and muttered something indistinct.

Hazard steepled his fingers and turned his gaze to Pressley. "You have this data siphon?"

"I can get it to you," she replied evenly, "once my sister is free."

Hazard shook his head. "You understand, I must see what is on the data siphon before I can commit to anything."

"All of my previous data siphons contained reliable info of value to you. I think you can trust this one does too. McCleary wouldn't have sent his cyborg enforcers after me if the data weren't legit."

"You'll have to give me something to go on here."

"All right." Pressley reached inside her shirt and pulled the siphon out of her bra. "Here it is. We can even watch the video if you must, though it's brutal. But I won't hand it over until my sister is safe. She's just a kid. She doesn't deserve to be involved in this at all."

"Perhaps not." He turned a glare on Malcolm again. "Do any of us deserve the terrible things that happen to us?"

Malcolm remained silent.

Hazard turned on a screen on the wall. "Show me."

Pressley activated the data siphon and connected it to the in-house system. "Don't watch," she whispered to her mother. "It's awful."

She brought up the incriminating video and let it play. She kept her own eyes averted. No way was she going to subject herself to that again. Her stomach was unhappy enough already with the smell of the food.

Halfway through, her mother took Pressley's hand, swearing under her breath.

"I warned you," Pressley murmured.

"You were right." She squeezed Pressley's hand.

When the video ended, silence reigned for several long seconds. Pressley lifted her eyes again. Bobby watched her with a troubled expression. She focused on Hazard. "You see? I was telling you the truth. He has to be stopped. You'll have all the info you need to bring him down and win the election. I'll have my sister back. It's a win-win. Now will you help us?" She tucked the data siphon away again.

Hazard barked out a harsh laugh. "For old time's sake, eh Malcolm?"

"For justice's sake," Malcolm said. "Do you still believe in justice, Hazard?"

Hazard snorted.

He had spoken about justice often enough in his campaign speeches. Was anything Hazard Snow said the truth?

Hazard gestured to his bodyguard.

Malcolm came to his feet.

Instinctively, Pressley dove beneath the table, dragging Mom with her. Heavy booted feet burst through the servers' entrance. Enforcers.

Gunshots exploded in the small space. Screams erupted from the diners downstairs. Mother screamed Malcolm's name. The table flew off them. Dishes and food clattered to the floor. Someone howled, and Pressley thought it was Hazard Snow.

"Run!" Malcolm commanded. Pressley scrambled up toward the sliding screen, hauling her mother by the arm. The cyborg enforcers were already rising from under the upended table.

Malcolm fired a couple more shots in their general direction to give Pressley and Mom enough time to get out. She didn't have a chance to see what had happened to Hazard. Or to Bobby or Gil. She didn't have a chance to worry about it.

Arm in arm with her mom, she barreled down the stairs into the crowd of panicked restaurant patrons bolting for the door or ducking under tables. Malcolm came right behind them. His handgun popped off shots in the direction of the enforcers, which barely even slowed them down. Whatever ethical programming existed in their cyborg brains must have prohibited them from firing into a crowd of innocents. But they were fast closing on Pressley and the others.

Malcolm tossed chairs and tables, even the maître d's podium to give them half a chance of getting out. The chaos overwhelming the sushi bar worked in their favor.

Pressley flew out the doors into the sweaty summer night, still clinging to her mother's arm. Lights and displays from all the surrounding buildings cast the streets in a neon glow nearly as bright as day. She spotted a nightclub a couple of doors down spilling music out onto the sidewalk. She made a run for it, pushing past the line of people waiting to get in, through the velvet rope blocking the door, shouldering her way past the bouncer, who protested until Malcolm barreled through, gun drawn.

The mob inside the club pulsed with the rhythm of the electronic dance music thumping from the speakers. Pressley pulled them into the middle of the mass. A thick miasma of various smokables coagulated in the air. Laser lights in every color danced across the smoke and lit up the writhing crowd.

"I'm going to be sick," Mom groaned.

Pressley thought so too, but they couldn't afford to stop and puke now. "Keep your head down and try to blend in."

"Blend in? Are you kidding?"

Mom was right about that. She and Malcolm in their work-on-the-farm clothes looked like sheep among jaguars—jaguars with holographic tats and multi-colored hair and revealing outfits. Malcolm's gun didn't help either.

"Keep moving," Malcolm said. The crush of dancers proved nearly impenetrable. Pressley wormed her way through. Bouncing and gyrating to the music made it easier to sink deeper into the crowd. She and Mom took turns gagging on the odors.

Shouts behind them announced the arrival of the enforcers. Pressley resisted the urge to turn around. Mother and Malcolm pressed close in behind her.

"Everybody clear out!" The enforcer's voice echoed over the driving beat of the music. Most of the patrons took no notice, too high to care.

"Don't look back," Malcolm said. "Head for the back room."

Pressley was already on her way there, so he must have been speaking to her mom. She reached back and took Mom's hand. The music cut off. "Clear the dance floor!" The enforcer had darkened his voice enough to send fear shivering through Pressley's bones. The dancing shuddered to a stop. A shot rang out. Pressley jumped and Mother squeezed her hand tighter. A light fixture crashed from the ceiling. The club patrons scattered like roaches, running for the exits and diving into booths and under tables.

Pressley sprinted for the back, crashing through a door marked *Employees Only*, praying the general chaos would hide their escape.

"There!" Malcolm bellowed.

Pressley couldn't see what he was pointing at, but she saw the exit door. A pile of garbage bags stood in front of it. She didn't miss a step. The garbage squished beneath her feet, releasing the stench of nightclub refuse. She pushed her way through the door, overcome by the smell, and retched onto the pavement in the relative dark and quiet of the alleyway between buildings.

"We can't stop," Malcolm murmured.

Pressley looked up to see her mom puking too, Malcolm's hand on her back. He was right. They had no time to linger.

"We should find the truck," Malcolm said.

"No. They'll be tracking the truck. We'll have to steal something."

"Steal a car?" Mom rasped. "You can't be serious."

"Pressley's right. It's the only way we're getting out of here alive."

"Malcolm!"

He took her by the shoulders. "Cars can be replaced, Annie. We can't."

"We're just borrowing it anyway," Pressley said. "We'll leave it someplace safe."

"You've done this before," Mom accused.

"Yes. Once. A couple of days ago—for the exact same reason. I don't plan on making it a habit. I'm not even sure I can pull it off again. It's not like I go around stealing cars all the time."

"Okay." Malcolm stepped between Pressley and her mother before they could get any more heated. "What do you need?"

"Preferably somewhere with other cars starting up nearby."

"All right. One of the valet lots, then."

"High probability enforcers will be searching all the lots nearby. We'll have to walk a ways."

"Are you up for that?" Malcolm asked Mom.

She wrapped her arms around herself. "I am if I need to be." She squared her jaw.

Their sprint from the sushi bar just now left Pressley's knees wobbly and her arms trembling. It had to be even harder on her mother, twenty years older. The thought of walking who knew how far with enforcers still after them made her want to curl up on the pavement and never get up.

"We have to move now," Malcolm said. Pressley could hear voices in the back room of the club getting louder. Enforcers would be back here any second.

"This way." Pressley motioned them away from the nightclub, farther down the alley, intending to lead them back onto the more crowded sidewalks, where she thought the enforcers wouldn't spot them immediately. She didn't want to find out who else might be lurking back here.

"Pressley!"

She nearly jumped out of her skin. Someone came running up the alley toward them. Malcolm held up his gun. "Stop right there."

"Bobby." A muddled rush of emotion swept through her. Relief, anger, affection, and fear in a jumble that misted up her eyes again. She ran into his arms. "What the hell, Bobby?"

"Thank God you're all right." He pulled her tight.

She stepped back and slapped him.

"Are you here to take us back to Hazard Snow? Because I will let Malcolm shoot you."

"No! I didn't know he had enforcers there. I didn't know anything. I got in touch with him through Gil. Hazard sent me a suit and told me to come, so I did. I wouldn't have put you in danger."

"You didn't know I was going to be there until you saw me."

"I didn't know, Press. I wouldn't have let you in there if I had. Believe me." He looked at the ground. "Gil Wang is dead. The enforcers shot him when he tried to run."

"Damn," Pressley muttered. He was a jerk, but he didn't deserve that.

"Go!" Malcolm bellowed. The back door of the nightclub had banged open.

"Over the wall," Pressley hissed. A half-wall of brick separated the narrow alley from the one behind. Pressley and Bobby scrambled over with Malcolm right behind. He turned to help his wife over, and they sprinted between darkened shops and onto the well-lit street beyond.

Pressley ducked into a small café.

"How many?" the hostess asked.

"Four." Pressley glanced behind them at the door. No sign of enforcers yet.

"It'll be about twenty minutes." The woman had an octopus tattooed on her face in purples and greens that wriggled against her cheeks.

"That will be fine," Pressley said. The little waiting area was packed with people.

"Name and phone number?" The hostess held up a little tablet to record the information.

"Annelise," Pressley said. Then she rattled off the number of Malcom's phone. He'd insisted she memorize it before they left the hotel.

"We'll text you when your table's ready."

"Great."

She moved to stand among the others waiting to get in. Her family huddled around her.

"Won't be long before the enforcers start searching each building," Malcolm said. Mother clung to his arm, pale and bedraggled.

"Do you have a car?" Pressley asked Bobby.

"Nope. Just a bike I borrowed off a buddy."

Because Pressley had taken his. It was still at her mother's farmstead. "That will do," she said.

"It won't hold us all."

"It doesn't have to." She addressed Malcolm. "Bobby and I will go get a car and meet you back here."

"Do we have to split up?" Mom asked. "Shouldn't we stick together?"

"We're more noticeable in a group. And besides, you look exhausted. I'll be quick. Promise."

Mom frowned, and Pressley guessed she was worrying about stealing a car again.

"With Bobby's help, I won't have to steal anything. I hope."

"Do whatever you have to. Just get us out of here," Malcolm said.

Mom nodded and wrapped Pressley in a hug. "Be careful."

"I will. And if you do get seated, order me some pecan pie to go." Her stomach rumbled at the thought of it.

"Pecan pie?" Mom gave her a quizzical look.

"What? You don't have any cravings?"

"At a time like this?"

Pressley shrugged. "Pregnancy is weird, isn't it?"

"Very."

Bobby plucked at her sleeve. "Let's go."

They went back outside. "Give me your suit coat," Pressley said. She slipped it over her shoulders. Not much as far as disguises, but she prayed it would be enough "How far away is the bike?"

"Just around the corner. By the sushi bar."

Pressley hooked her arm through his and kept her head down as they made their way down the street. It wasn't as crowded as she'd hoped, but enough people were out and about to give the enforcers at least a little trouble picking her out from among the rest. Hopefully, it would buy her enough time.

"Bae, you believe me, don't you? I would never put you in danger."

"I know, Bobby. I believe you."

"Because I love you, Press. I really do. I'm not going to abandon you."

"Thank you," she said softly. "That…means a lot."

He kissed her cheek. She blinked fiercely against the sudden tears. "Let's get this mess taken care of, then we can figure out the rest, okay?"

"Okay."

They rounded the corner onto La Cienega. A dozen cop cars blocked the road in front of the sushi bar. The red and blue lights cast a lurid glow over the street.

"Will we be able to get to the bike?"

"I think so."

They moved into the press of people hovering around the sushi bar. Some were injured, being treated by emergency personnel. Some gave statements to police officers. Others stood around gawking. Pressley kept her head down, fearing someone from the restaurant would recognize her as the woman who'd crashed through them with a crazy gunman and cyborg enforcers right behind. Better to stick with the gawkers on the edge.

She spotted an enforcer prowling the perimeter of cop cars. "Careful," she whispered.

"He's right in front of the bike."

Pressley swore. "We'll stay right here until he moves."

They stood at the edge of the crowd as if trying to get a look at what was going on, keeping one eye on the position of the enforcer.

"That woman keeps staring at us," Bobby whispered.

Pressley glanced in the direction he nodded. Crap. The woman was looking right at them, her face wrinkled in concentration.

"Kiss me," she whispered.

Bobby obliged, his hands cradling her cheeks to further obscure her face. She kept her eyes open. The woman hurried toward one of the cops. Pressley broke the kiss. "We gotta go. She can ID me."

"Enforcer's moving away," Bobby said. He grabbed her hand, and they jogged toward the bike, trying not to look in too big of a hurry. They passed behind the back of the enforcer. Bobby pointed to the charging stall where the bike waited. A glance over her shoulder revealed the woman talking to a cop, pointing to where Pressley and Bobby had been standing but clearly unaware of where they had gone. It wouldn't take long to spot them.

"Let's go."

Bobby climbed on the bike and Pressley got on behind. She wrapped her arms tight around him and leaned against his back. He pulled the bike out onto the street and steered it away from the cops and the chaos. "Where to?" he asked.

"Wherever the valets took Malcolm's truck." She had an idea for getting it back without it being IDed immediately.

"Yeah, I know the place."

That was one benefit of Bobby's Uber job. He knew where almost everything in L.A. was. The valet lot was half a mile away from the restaurant. They pulled the bike up to one corner and checked for enforcers (thankfully absent). Pressley used her burner to grab a gate code from one of the valets. A couple of minutes later, they were parked next to Malcolm's gray pickup.

She climbed into the driver's seat, and Bobby got in the passenger side. He left the bike idling beside them at Pressley's request.

"Your dad's a real badass."

"He's not my dad." Pressley started the truck and popped open the user interface panel. "He's my mom's husband. I didn't know he existed before yesterday."

"He sure is protective for someone who just met you."

"Yeah." Her fingers flew over the little keyboard. "Kind of nice to know somebody like that has my back." She shrugged. "Even if it's just because he loves my mother."

"I wish I had a dad like that."

"I don't even know my real dad. Not even his name." She was only half-listening, changing the truck's ID to match the bike's and vice versa.

"It won't be that way for our baby," Bobby said.

Pressley looked over, not sure what to say.

"I mean—even if we don't…" He trailed off. "I want to be there for them. I want to be a better father than my own." He looked down at his hands. "If I can."

Pressley laid a hand on his arm. "I'm sure you can."

He smiled at that. He looked as young as Twiggy, which—hell—he almost was. Only twenty-one. She shouldn't have put him in this position.

"You can turn off the bike," she said, letting her eyes slide away from him. "We'll have to leave it here for now. The enforcers will think Malcolm's truck hasn't moved." At least, she hoped they wouldn't. If they checked it visually, she'd be screwed.

"Hector won't be happy about that."

"It won't be for long. I hope. As soon as we clear up this mess, he can come get it. It'll be safe here."

Bobby nodded, still looking unhappy about it.

"Your bike's at my mom's. We can get it back, too, once this is over."

Not that she had any idea what they were supposed to do now that Hazard Snow's help was off the table.

She entered the address of the café, and the truck pulled out of the lot and onto the street. Anyone who actually checked the ID would know right away it was supposed to be a bike, not a pickup, but she hoped to be back at the ratty hotel before that happened.

"Text Malcolm and tell him we're coming. We'll pick them up outside the café."

"Sure." He was quiet for a minute, typing out the message on his burner.

Pressley pulled into traffic. Bobby pocketed the phone. "I thought you and your mom didn't get along."

"I thought so too." She eased into the turning lane to take them back to the café. "But she's like a different person. Maybe getting married mellowed her out." Who knew how long that would last. She hesitated then added, "My mom is pregnant also."

"Really? That's weird."

"I know, right?" She chuckled. "That's what I keep saying." She sighed. "But who knows what will happen when this is all over." Especially if they couldn't save Twiggy. She didn't even want to think about that.

"I wonder if my family would all come rushing to my aid if I were the one in trouble." He frowned. "Doubt it."

"You might be surprised." Pressley certainly had been.

Mom and Malcolm were waiting right outside the café. Pressley pulled the truck up to the curb and they climbed in, Malcolm in the driver's seat and Mom on the other side with Pressley and Bobby squished in between in a cab that barely held three. Mom passed Pressley a cardboard takeout box with a piece of warm pecan pie in it.

"Thank you," she sighed and wolfed it down as they drove away. Then she leaned against Bobby's shoulder and closed her eyes until Bobby shook her gently awake sometime later.

Malcolm had brought them to a different, older, even seedier motel. Layers of graffiti decorated the outside walls, and trash littered the nearly empty parking lot. Not quite empty, though. An illicit drug deal looked to be going down in one dark corner. From the upper floor came the sounds of shouting and objects being thrown. Funny how she actually felt safer out here. They were clear out in Pasadena now.

Span Corp Tower was nothing but a spike of glittering lights in the distance.

They got a room on the corner of the third floor with two double beds that at least had clean sheets on them. The room smelled of must and old tobacco, but nothing worse.

"I'll take the floor," Bobby said in an apparent attempt at gallantry. Pressley rolled her eyes. "You don't have to do that."

"Not like you can get her any more pregnant than she already is, kid," Malcolm said. "Might as well take the bed."

Bobby flushed crimson at that, and Mom's face turned disapproving. Pressley was too tired to care. She climbed between the covers. A minute later, Bobby slid in beside her. She had to admit, his presence was comforting.

She awoke late into the night to the sound of her mother quietly weeping. She pushed herself up. Malcolm was awake too, sitting up with one hand on her mother's shuddering back. In the other, he held the automatic rifle he'd taken off the dead enforcer in his kitchen. Only Bobby was still asleep, breathing deep and even. Malcolm put a finger to his lips. Pressley nodded and lay back down. Only a few minutes later, she drifted off again.

. . .

The famous SoCal sunshine streamed in through the window when Pressley woke up again. Mom and Malcolm sat at the little round table in the corner eating breakfast. They must have ordered in. Bobby stirred and sat up beside her, stretching and groggy.

"Have some," Mom said.

Pressley grabbed a wrapped breakfast burrito off the table and sat cross-legged on the bed. Her stomach pinched painfully, but luckily the eggs and sausage and hashbrowns went down okay. Bobby took the breakfast sandwich Mother offered and sat beside her.

"So," Pressley began around a mouthful of breakfast, "was Hazard Snow working for Ransom McCleary all along, you think?"

"I suspect McCleary made him an offer he couldn't refuse in order to find out what you had and to get it from you."

That made sense. She nodded thoughtfully. "Malcolm, what did happen in Hong Kong, if you don't mind me asking?"

Malcolm's face turned stony. "I do mind, actually. I can't tell you how glad I am I didn't have to make it public."

"Right. I'm sorry."

He waved off the apology.

"And in case you're wondering," Mom said, "yes, he has told me about it. It's in the past and there's no need to repeat it. It's like that video." She shivered. "So awful."

"I did warn you not to watch it." Pressley took another bite.

"You were right. I'll never get that out of my head. That poor girl."

"She deserves justice," Pressley said. "And everyone forced out onto the streets deserves justice." She huffed out her breath. "Have you ever wondered where he finds the men to turn into enforcers?"

"Prisons," Malcolm said grimly. "Homeless camps. Men desperate enough to give up their identity to make a buck. A lot of them are war veterans."

Pressley nodded, thinking of the man with the claw.

"How sad." Mother shook her head. "I assume there's a reason we can't just turn all of it over to police?"

"In L.A.? No way. They'd arrest me for illegal hacking and the video would disappear forever."

"McCleary is king in L.A.," Bobby said.

Pressley looked out the window toward Span Corp Tower in the distance, lights chasing around it even in the sunshine. "We'll have to go in ourselves, find Twiggy, and get her out. Then we expose Ransom McCleary. Hazard Snow too."

"How will we do that?" Mom asked. "Without the cops or Hazard Snow's help."

"We have him." Bobby nodded at Malcolm.

"True." Mom patted his arm affectionately.

Malcolm squeezed her hand. "I don't know that I'm the hero you all think I am. I'll do what I can."

"The only real leverage we have is the data siphon," Pressley said.

"We can't exchange that for Twiggy. It wouldn't be right," Mom said, her voice strained. "As much as we might want to."

"No, we can't give it to McCleary. He'd kill Twiggy anyway, and the rest of us."

They fell silent. Pressley nibbled the inside of her lip. There had to be a way. She wasn't about to simply abandon Twiggy to Ransom McCleary. Chances were she was somewhere inside Span Corp Tower. An idea began to percolate in her brain.

"Maybe…maybe we can kill two birds with one stone. If I can get into Span Corp without getting caught, I can find out where Twiggy is being held and get her out, plus expose McCleary's crime."

"What is your plan, then?" Malcolm asked.

Pressley kept her voice low. "I'm already deep into the system at Span Corp. Cybersecurity won't have found everything. I can find out where they're holding Twiggy and get to her. Once I do, I'll release the video."

"Release it?" Mom asked.

"Yes. Broadcast it everywhere Span Corp can reach. On all the building displays, phones, TVs—everything. The cops won't be able to ignore it or suppress it then."

"But it's awful!"

"I agree. It's sickening. But I don't know what else to do. While Ransom McCleary deals with getting arrested, I can sneak out with Twiggy."

"That could work," Malcolm said. "If you think you can get that vid past the censors."

"Leave that to me," Pressley said. "I can circumvent the censors. We just need a plan for getting in and out of Span Corp Tower.

"With the enforcers looking for us?" Mother said. "I don't know…" Her eyes misted over.

Malcolm put his arm around her protectively, a gesture that put an unaccountable lump in Pressley's throat.

"We can work around that," Malcolm said. "With some careful planning."

"Right," Pressley said. "So let's get started."

IV.

A few hours later, an Uber dropped them off a couple of blocks from Span Corp Tower—minus Bobby, who had gone home to change into his uniform and rent another bike. The fact that neither Hazard nor McCleary knew he was with them should work in his favor. Pressley wore a ruffled, floral skirt and white midi top with dark, wraparound, tech-enabled glasses they'd had delivered to the hotel. Her mom had given her a passable pixie cut, and they'd dyed her hair a deep blue-black. She looked about as unlike herself as she could manage. Mom and Malcolm had changed into touristy Hawaiian shirts and shorts. Malcolm had shaved and dyed the gray out of his hair. Pressley hoped the disguises, along with her facial recognition hacking, would be enough to get her through the front door of Span Corp Tower. She pulled out the burner and held it wrapped in her fist. Bobby couldn't have made the delivery this fast, but she wanted to be ready when he did. A quick check of the area around them assured them that they hadn't been followed.

Traffic buzzed down the road beside them. People flowed along the sidewalk in a steady stream on foot or hoverboards or motorized skates. Most of them wore tech glasses or watched their phones. Most of them didn't care about the abuses of Span Corp or put up with them for the sake of convenience and not having to think for themselves.

"How long have you and Bobby been together?" Mom asked her.

"A few months." She waited for further interrogation, but Mom simply nodded and fell silent. Pressley had questions of her own—like why had Mom decided to carry and raise her and Twiggy alone? What kind of relationship had she had with their fathers? Why hadn't either of them ever come around to see their girls? Did Mom ever regret her choices? Maybe she'd regretted letting them both move to the city— not that Pressley or Twiggy had given Mom much say in the matter. How did one raise a child anyway?

Now didn't seem like the best time to ask. She hoped she'd get a chance to ask her later.

Mother leaned against Malcolm, staring wistfully up at Span Corp Tower. "Hang on, Twiggy. We're coming."

She spoke under her breath, but Pressley heard it and her heart pinched tight. The three of them against all the might of Ransom McCleary. And maybe Hazard Snow too. Hard to muster any hope, but she had to try. Poor Twiggy. And poor Mom. A memory surfaced of the day Pressley had moved out for good. After she and her mother had finished their shouting match and Pressley had stormed out of the house with all her belongings in a duffel bag, Twiggy had chased her sobbing down the lane, begging Pressley not to leave her there alone. At the time, Pressley had hugged her little sister and told her she was sorry but she couldn't stay. She'd promised to keep in touch, but as Twiggy hadn't been allowed a phone, she hadn't. Which was why Twiggy's arrival in L.A. four years later had been such a shock.

"Pressley," Malcolm nudged her out of her reverie and nodded toward a young black man hustling down the sidewalk, craning his neck around frantically. "That him?"

She pushed the tech glasses onto her head and waved her arm. "Corny! Over here."

He came puffing over, sweat beading on his forehead. He had the paper note she'd written clutched in one fist. "Pressley, girl, look at you! What happened to you? They had *enforcers* asking about you."

"I know. I'm sorry."

"What's going on?" He waved the note at her. "What's with all this cloak and dagger stuff?"

She grinned thinly. She'd hidden the note in a box of cookies that Bobby had delivered. It read, *Corny, I need your help. Meet me at the corner by Jaxie's ASAP. Don't bring your phone. Love, Press*

"Thanks for coming so fast."

"Well, yeah. I mean, are you okay?" He wrapped her in a bear hug.

"I'm okay. Corny, this is my mom, Annelise, and her husband, Malcolm."

"Pleased to meet you." Corny shook their hands. "So, you gonna tell me what's going on?"

"My younger daughter, Pressley's sister, is being held hostage in Span Corp Tower," Mom said.

"Wha—?" He gaped at Pressley and her mother. "Span Corp Tower isn't a prison."

"Yes, it is, Corny." Pressley laid her hand on his arm. "And not just for the employees. You know that."

Corny pressed his lips shut, folding his arms across his chest.

"You left your phone, like I asked?"

"Yeah."

"Good. Will you help me, Corny?"

"Press—" He glanced around as if expecting enforcers to materialize out of the crowd. Not an unjustified fear, actually.

"No one's listening," she assured him.

His chest heaved. He glanced around again and folded his arms, looked at the ground, the traffic, the buildings, and finally back at Pressley.

"Yeah, I'll help you. You know I will."

"Thank you, my friend."

Corny nodded. His stance relaxed a little. "Tell me."

Pressley quietly explained the truth of her employment at Span Corp and what she had uncovered. "He took my sister to get the data siphon back, but if he does get it, he'll kill us both."

Corny opened his mouth and shut it again without making a sound.

"What I need from you is easy," Pressley said.

Corny gave her an incredulous look.

"Really easy," she assured him. "I just need you to get the three of us into the building. Then I need you to take a little break. Lunch hour or whatever. Head to the atrium and enjoy your cookies. Simple, right? And if you just happened to accidentally leave your computer unlocked, well, that's just an honest mistake, right?"

Corny closed his eyes and tipped his head back. "You know what could happen to me."

"I'll make sure it doesn't. You can log in with this dummy account." She passed him a slip of paper with the credentials written down. "No one will know you were involved. Please. My sister's life is on the line here."

Corny studied the paper and nodded slowly. "Okay. I'll do it." He gave her a look of exasperated fondness.

"Thank you, Corny. I won't forget this. Ever."

"Oh, stop." He shook his head with a weak sort of chuckle. "I better get back."

"We'll be right behind you."

"And take a break. Got it." His coffee-brown forehead wrinkled. "McCleary really killed someone?"

"Yeah, he did."

Corny shuddered. "I wish you luck, my friend." He hugged her again and hurried back down the sidewalk.

He seems a little jumpy," Malcolm said quietly. "You sure he won't panic and turn us in?"

Pressley considered the question. "He is nervous. Frightened. But he's been a good friend since we started working together, and he trusts me." She shook her head. "He won't deliberately betray us."

"Okay," Malcolm said. "Let's go. But try and keep your friend out of trouble."

"That's the plan."

Pressley's stomach fluttered as they approached the main entrance to Span Corp Tower. She usually came in through the parking garage. The twelve-foot-tall revolving glass doors facing the street were a lot more imposing.

Mom tucked her arm through Malcolm's and they stepped inside. Pressley followed, trying not to flinch or look like she was trying to hide. At least there weren't wanted posters flashing on the walls. McCleary probably wanted to keep everything hushed up as much as he could.

The front lobby was all glass and chrome with two-story screens playing Span Corp ads and the same nature scenes that played outside. Natural sunlight filtered down through massive skylights three stories up. Their footsteps echoed on the tiled floor.

The desk itself formed a half-circle in front of a bank of elevators. Three holographic AI receptionists manned the desk, maintaining a smooth flow of people in and out. A well-furnished waiting area filled the space between the door and the desk. Bobby sat in one of the chairs, thumbing through a magazine and studiously ignoring Pressley and her parents. She felt a zing of relief at the sight of him. So far, so good.

"Welcome to Span Corp," the receptionist said perkily when they reached the front of the line. "How may I assist you today?"

"Daisy Ruiz, please," Malcolm said—the dummy name she'd given Corny.

"One moment."

Pressley held her breath.

"Elevator six," the receptionist said. "Floor 121, hall C." Three visitor chits emerged from a slot in the desk. "Keep those on you at all times inside Span Corp Tower. Have a wonderful day."

They each took a chit and headed for the indicated elevator. Pressley turned as the doors closed and caught Bobby's eyes for a split second.

We should place the baby for adoption, she thought. She knew at once that would break his heart. Her hand came instinctively to rest against her belly. This wasn't the time to be thinking about that.

"Sick?" Mom whispered.

Pressley shook her head. "Just thinking."

"Let's talk," Mom said. "When we're done here."

"Yeah." As if they were just going to be here for a short business transaction.

She collected the visitor chits from Mom and Malcolm. "Head for the atrium on ten. Lots of employees hang out there on break. I'll alert you when I'm with Twiggy." Then they could put the rest of the pieces into place.

The elevator stopped, and Mom and Malcolm got off. Mom hugged her. "Be careful, okay?"

"You too."

The elevator slid upward again and a few minutes later, the doors opened on floor 121, her workplace up until a few days ago. Luckily, everyone was in their cubes, heads down, working. She doubted her disguise would hold up with any actual co-workers. She hustled toward C hall and Corny's cube next to her own.

It wasn't hers anymore, though. Someone else sat at the desk, tech glasses on, drumming her fingers on the desk. Pressley didn't stop to watch the newcomer. Business as usual for Span Corp. *Never forget just how replaceable you are.*

She slipped into Corny's cube and blacked the walls. He'd left his computer up just as she'd asked. "Thank you, Corny." She pulled up a chair and accessed his terminal. First things first—find Twiggy and get to her, then post the video.

Her skin crawled at the thought of the horrible scene playing on all the screens in the lobby, outside a hundred feet high on the side of the building, on a billion phones around the world. But it had to be done.

She attached the data siphon to the inside of Corny's desk drawer and uploaded the video for quick release. Then she accessed the company system.

She brought up the schematics of the tower—cubicles, offices, cafeterias, atriums, gyms, healthcare facilities, and so on. None of it was helpfully labeled "detention" or "dungeon" or "place we keep illegally detained hostages." Security cams in areas she thought most likely didn't yield any results either.

The burner buzzed in her pocket. Bobby.

Hazard Snow wants to see me. He asked me to meet him here.

Snow here? At Span Corp Tower? Maybe that wasn't so surprising given what had happened last night. *Does he know you're here?*

I don't think so.

Did he give you a room number? I can bring up the security feed.

Level 303. Suite 7.

She accessed the camera. There he was, sitting behind a polished mahogany desk, talking on his phone, looking like he owned the world. Her teeth clenched. If Bobby refused, it might seem suspicious.

Wait a few minutes, she sent. *Go see him, but tread carefully. He knows what you saw last night. Call Corny's extension, and I'll be able to hear you.*

Okay.

Be careful.

I will.

A few minutes later, the call request appeared on Corny's desktop. Pressley answered.

"Can you hear me okay?" Bobby asked, his voice muffled by his pocket.

"Yeah. Muting myself now."

On the security feed, Hazard Snow ended his phone call and straightened his coat, checked the time, drummed his fingers on his desk, and cast hooded glances at the office door, waiting for Bobby to arrive.

Pressley could relate. Her breathing quickened like she was running a marathon. Nausea built up in her stomach. She reached for the soda crackers in her pocket and munched nervously, choking a little on the crumbs.

"I love you," Bobby said through the phone, and she choked in earnest, spraying crumbs across Corny's desk. She grabbed an open can of Coke he'd left and guzzled down a swig.

"I won't let you down," Bobby said.

"I know you won't," she said around the coughing, though Bobby couldn't hear her.

He knocked. Hazard Snow stood. A smile oozed across his face. He opened the door and ushered Bobby inside. Pressley watched like a fly on the ceiling.

"Bobby, thank you for coming. Please have a seat." He pulled out a sleek, silver chair in front of his desk.

"I have a lot of deliveries to make," Bobby said.

Pressley chuckled. "You tell him, Bobby."

"You don't have to worry about deliveries anymore," Hazard said. "You work for me now." He sat in his high-backed office chair and motioned for Bobby to sit too.

Bobby stayed standing. "Doing what, exactly?"

"Anything I ask you to." His voice turned hard. "And don't worry. You'll be well-compensated. Far better than a delivery boy's earnings."

Was this a bribe or a threat?

"Will it involve getting shot at? Because—"

"Sit down, Mr. Wilds."

Bobby sat.

Pressley held her breath and downed another cracker.

"I assure you," Hazard said. "I will do everything in my power to ensure your safety."

"Sure, you will," Pressley muttered.

"I must apologize for last night. I had no idea Malcolm Burke would prove to be such a danger."

"You're the one who brought enforcers," Pressley hissed and willed her stomach to behave.

"It is important that we find him," Hazard said. "Before he hurts anyone else."

The liar. Pressley fists shook. To think she'd ever believed in Hazard Snow.

"That video—" Bobby said.

"Yes." Hazard shook his head. "Horrible. Truly. Trust me, Bobby. Once I'm elected governor, I can deal with Ransom McCleary. Until that time…" He lowered his voice almost beyond Pressley's hearing. "I have a fine line to tread. You're going to have to trust me on this for a little while."

Bobby nodded wordlessly.

"Good. You see, Bobby, working with me is the only way I can guarantee your safety and well-being, you understand. Without that protection, well—I can't say what might happen."

And there was the threat.

Bobby didn't speak or even move. Pressley couldn't see the expression on his face, but whatever it was, it satisfied Hazard Snow. He leaned back in his exec's chair and steepled his fingers. "Here's what I need you to do."

Corny stepped into the cube. Pressley put a finger to her lips before he could say anything.

"This girl. Pressley Pierce. You two are close?" Hazard asked.

Pressley held her breath.

"Press, I gotta get back to work," Corny said in a stage whisper.

"Shhh."

Bobby shrugged. "We dated, but she hasn't talked to me much lately."

"She asked you to get in touch with me."

"Oh, my goodness." Corny leaned over Pressley's shoulder. "Is that—?"

"Corny, hush."

"I've always been her only point of contact with you, except for Gil, of course, but..."

"Yes, I see. Do you think you could contact her now? Find out where she is?"

"I doubt she'll talk to me after last night."

"Press," Corny hissed in her ear. "What the—"

"Shhh."

He laid his hand on her shoulder, but he stayed quiet.

"I don't know how," Bobby said. "She doesn't have a phone anymore. It was her father who called me yesterday."

"Call him then." Hazard was beginning to sound testy. "So long as you find out where they are and get the data siphon from them."

"You know, Pressley'd trust me a lot more if I could tell her where her sister is."

"Yes, I'm sure she would."

"Do you know where her sister is?"

"Come on. Tell him," Pressley whispered.

"Just get me that siphon. Do or say whatever you have to. Whatever you want. You do see the importance of this, don't you?"

"Yes, sir."

"Good." Hazard stood and showed Bobby the door. "Don't let me down."

"I won't."

Bobby closed the door behind him. Hazard stood with his hands on his hips for second before returning to his desk and picking up his phone again. She disconnected the call.

"Pressley." Corny squeezed her shoulder. "Damn, girl. What the hell?"

She shook her head. "Don't ask and don't worry about me." She kissed his cheek. "You're an angel. Thank you, a million times over."

"You're…welcome?"

"If anyone asks, you haven't seen me."

"Gotcha. You take care of yourself."

"Oh, I will." She smiled. Her queasiness increased. She picked up the half-empty Coke bottle. "Can I take this?" She winced.

"Sure."

She hugged him one last time, and, checking the hallway for enforcers, stepped out of the cubicle. For a second, she felt a twinge of guilt for leaving the data siphon in his desk drawer, but it seemed highly unlikely anyone would look for it there.

She called Bobby on her burner when she was certain she was alone.

"Where are you headed?"

"Tenth-floor atrium."

"I'll meet you on the way."

She got into the elevator, frowning. She still had no idea where Twiggy was and no clue how to find out. She had the feeling even Hazard Snow didn't know where Twiggy was being held.

Bobby got on the elevator on the fifty-sixth floor. "Man, I was nervous. I thought I was going to barf." He leaned his head against the wall with his eyes closed.

"Yeah?" She swallowed down the last of the Coke. "Welcome to my world."

"Oh, Press." He straightened. "I'm sorry. You must be miserable."

"Yeah, a little." She shrugged. For a few awkward seconds, they looked at each other with a thousand things left unsaid between them.

Bobby took her hand. Pressley took a step closer to him, and a heartbeat later, she was in his arms.

The tears came against her wishes—stupid hormones. They dripped against Bobby's shoulder.

"Don't cry, bae," he whispered. "We'll be okay."

There was no logical way he could promise her that. No way he could reasonably make it okay. But for some reason, it comforted her anyway. *We'll be okay.*

She wanted it to be true. She moved her hand to the back of his neck, pulling him closer, and felt something small and hard stuck to the back of his collar like a metal tick.

"Bobby!" She yanked it free. Just a tiny, silver disk, barely the size of her fingertip.

Bobby swore.

"Tracker?"

"Hazard," Bobby said. "And now he knows where we are." And probably where they were headed too.

Pressley dropped the tracker to the floor and ground it under her heel, but the damage was already done.

"Stop the elevator."

Bobby hit the red emergency button and the elevator stopped with a slight jerk.

She texted Malcolm. *Get out now. They know we're here.*

The elevator shuddered and started down again. No matter how many times Pressley jammed her thumb into the emergency button, it wouldn't stop.

"Have any weapons?" Bobby asked.

"No." They'd never have been able to sneak guns into Span Corp Tower.

"Where's the data siphon?"

"I hid it."

"Good." Bobby grabbed her hand. "We'll make a run for it."

That wouldn't work. Pressley's heart raced and her stomach churned. Maybe puking on the enforcers would distract them.

"Bobby, you have to make Hazard believe you were trying to get the siphon from me."

The elevator sighed to a stop. Pressley squeezed Bobby's hand.

The doors slid open. Two cyborg enforcers stood shoulder to shoulder, blocking the exit. Pressley lunged forward. Her shoulder slammed into an enforcer's mid-section. A grunt of pain whooshed out of her. The man—if he could be called that—was an immovable rock. He grabbed her wrist and wrenched her arm painfully behind her. She cried out as he twisted her other arm around and handcuffed them together. "Bobby!"

"I work for Hazard Snow," Bobby shouted. "Let me go."

The enforcer marched Pressley forward. The cold steel of a handgun pressed against the back of her head. She stumbled, and he yanked her up violently.

Bobby continued to shout about working for Hazard. She hoped they'd believe him. She hoped Hazard believed him. Most of all, she hoped she could believe him, though it seemed likely that it wouldn't matter anymore in a few minutes.

Her stomach gave up, which didn't faze the enforcer in the slightest. Vomit spattered against her bare leg and dribbled down her chin. She coughed and choked, shaking her head to try and clear the puke off. The enforcer cuffed her with his gun.

The hallway he forced her down was stark and bare, strictly utilitarian. Harsh fluorescent lighting cast the gray walls and white tile in stark shadows. There were few doors along the sides and no windows. He pulled her up short in front of an unmarked metal door with no visible handle. It slipped open into the wall by means Pressley couldn't see. Her captor shoved her through the door, and with her hands bound, she couldn't keep from stumbling to her knees. She grunted at the impact.

The enforcer came to stand in front of her. The door slid shut again with a heavy thud. Pressley's stomach heaved and she puked again. The enforcer took a step back to keep it off of his shoes.

"Give me the data siphon."

"My hands are tied."

He didn't even blink. "Tell me where it is, and I'll get it off you."

"I don't have it."

"I will give you one more chance, Ms. Pierce. Where is the siphon?"

She lifted her chin to look him in the face, heart racing. "I don't have it. I got scared and I wiped it and threw it in the incinerator."

The enforcer didn't speak. The stony expression on his face didn't change. He dragged her to her feet and released the cuffs. A momentary rush of relief washed over her, at least until he stripped her clothes off and searched her body in the most painful and demeaning manner she could imagine. He made sure to be thorough, despite the fact that she puked twice more during the process.

Freezing and humiliated, she wrapped her arms around her chest. The floor beneath her bare feet was icy and slick with her vomit and urine she hadn't been able to control during the violation. A violent shivering overtook her, causing her teeth to clack together until her jaw ached. She kept her eyes on the floor.

The enforcer pawed through her clothes on a small table by the wall—the only piece of furniture in the room. He pocketed the burner and her soda crackers. Finding nothing more, he stepped in front of her again. "Where is it?"

"I…I…" The shivering stole her breath.

The enforcer's thick fist connected with her gut. She doubled over, retching from an empty stomach. The next blow came to the side of her head, and she dropped into the vomit and curled in on herself.

"Where is it?"

"I threw it away," she mumbled. *Be brave. For Twiggy. For the dead girl. For everyone.*

He kicked her with his heavy boot. Pain radiated from her knee up and down her leg. She cried out.

"Where is it?"

She couldn't answer, sobbing and shivering, her throat clenched. *Stay. Strong.*

The sharp sting of a lash or maybe a belt fell across her back. She curled up tighter. The lash fell across her bare skin over and over, until the enforcer yanked her head up by her hair and growled in her face.

"Where is it?"

She clenched her chattering teeth. *Brave. Strong. For Twiggy.* "I don't—I—I don't—I threw it away."

"Where?" He jerked her head farther back.

"Forty—fort—forty-third floor."

He dropped her head. She curled inward again. His footsteps retreated. The door slid open and shut again. Pressley didn't move until she was sure the enforcer was gone.

Still shaking, she used the wall to pull herself to her feet. Her clothes were still there in a heap on the little table. Thank goodness for that. She hobbled the few steps across the room on her aching knee and put them back on—a laborious and painful process. She had to rest, panting, in between each bit of clothing—

panties, then bra, shirt, skirt, sandals. The clothes stung her welts from the lashes, and she felt blood seeping through the back of the shirt. She was covered in her own vomit and urine, but at least she wasn't naked.

After what felt like half an hour of getting herself dressed, she limped to the door, leaning on the table and then the wall to keep herself up. The panel wouldn't open for her, of course. She hadn't expected it to. But if she could hack into it, she could get herself out. Or find out what happened to Bobby. And Mom and Malcolm. Or do…something. Anything but wait around to be executed.

Her thoughts slid away from her. She couldn't quite figure out what to do with the door panel. She had to close her eyes when the room started to spin, and the nausea seemed more intense than before. She sucked in a breath, rested her head against the wall. Just for a second, until she could see clearly again and be certain she wasn't going to puke.

The door opened. Pressley choked on a gasp, stumbled back, and fell on her bottom. An enforcer—the same one or someone different—hauled her up and hand-cuffed her again.

He marched her down the hall back toward the elevator, sending fiery stabs of pain through her sore knee. With his iron grip around her arm, she had no choice but to keep pace with him.

I'm going to die. Why he didn't just finish her off right now was a mystery. Maybe he was taking her somewhere where the clean-up would be easier. Throw her in a dumpster first then shoot her. Or maybe he was taking her to the clinic where they'd do her in humanely with lethal injection.

Not likely.

But whatever the case, she knew she would die. Her baby would die. And Twiggy. And quite possibly Bobby and Mom and Malcolm and their baby too. Her entire family. Family she hadn't even known she had a few days ago. Tears slid down her cheeks, and she could not wipe them away. She sniffed and the enforcer gave her an ugly sneer.

Up and up the elevator ascended, and Pressley realized they were going to the top—all the way up to Ransom McCleary's private penthouse. Her heart kicked up a gear. *That* might be even worse than death.

Brave, she reminded herself. *Strong.* She wasn't dead yet. She set her jaw, leaned over, and wiped her nose on the enforcer's sleeve. He pulled his arm away with a grunt and backhanded her across the cheek. That stung, but the blow only hardened her resolve. She stood up straighter. At the very least, she would spit in Ransom McCleary's face before she died.

Maybe she wouldn't change the world as she'd hoped. Maybe there wasn't anything decent people could do about the evil in the world. Maybe it was a mistake to try. But she would try anyway. She would die trying. She balled her bound hands into determined fists. She would die trying, and that was enough.

The elevator at last came to a stop. The enforcer locked his hand around her elbow again. The door opened to a quiet hallway with wood-paneled walls and plush, red carpeting.

The enforcer hauled her out faster than her sore knee wanted to go, over to a door at the far end of the hall about fifty feet away.

Another enforcer stood guard there like an oversized doorman in mirrored tech glasses. He stepped aside, and the door swung open on its own with a soft chime.

The enforcer pulled her inside an opulent living room. White leather semi-circle couches mirrored the curve of the walls. They faced a bank of windows that could no doubt be converted to viewscreens at a touch. A few minimalist coffee tables sat in front of the couches adorned with vases of flowers, e-readers, and holo-displays of foreign cities and stunning vistas.

A few round columns marked the edge of the sitting area. A lighted cascade of water ran down the length of each column into hidden catch basins below—an ostentatious show of waste. A huge round tank of glowing jellyfish floated lackadaisically in the middle of the columns. Beyond that, Pressley spotted a bar and a dining area, where a couple of women sat sipping drinks. Neither turned around to look at her when the enforcer brought her inside.

The man himself—Ransom McCleary—stood with his back to Pressley and the enforcer, looking out over the panoramic view of Los Angeles through the floor-to-ceiling windows. He was tall, broad-shouldered, and heavyset. He was mostly bald, with no trace of gray in his remaining hair despite being in his sixties. Pressley could see his face reflected in the window—neat, black beard, thin mustache, and an angry frown. Just like in the horrible video.

Terror gripped her throat at the memory of the savagery she had witnessed in him. She didn't want to die. Not like that.

The enforcer marched her up within the ring of couches. This could be it. The last moment of her life. She wanted to puke. It would serve him right to have vomit all over his pristine white carpet. McCleary turned to face her, and despite her brain screaming at her to run, she didn't flinch. Didn't lower her gaze. A horrible trembling engulfed her, but she clenched her teeth, balled her fists, and stood straight.

"You've caused a lot of trouble for me, young lady," Ransom said.

Pressley held her tongue, though she wanted to point out he'd done the same to her.

"You claim to have thrown away your data siphon?"

Again, she made no answer.

"It doesn't matter. Even if you hid it somewhere, whatever you think you found will never be made public. Make no mistake about that."

Pressley lifted her chin.

Ransom McCleary took three steps toward her. She would have retreated had the enforcer not been holding her in place.

Ransom loomed over her, so close she could smell the spicy tang of his breath. It ignited the nausea all over again. Her skin itched where she already had puke dried onto it.

Ransom grabbed her chin and turned her head from side to side, inspecting her. A shudder of revulsion rippled through her. McCleary ran his hands over her breasts. She hissed, and he leered at her. He walked around her, looking her over like some piece of furniture he wanted to buy. Pressley lowered her head. She would have spit in his face as she'd resolved, but her mouth had gone bone dry.

"A little old, but she'll do," McCleary announced from behind her. "Put her with the others."

Others? A sickening realization of his intentions hit her right in the gut.

McCleary left the room. The enforcer led her back out into the hall, past the guard and the elevator to another door at the opposite end, also guarded. The enforcer at the door stepped aside, and her captor knocked. That surprised her. The door wasn't keyed to let enforcers in. A few seconds later, a young woman opened the door. She was tall and thin and carried herself like a dancer. Her skin was deep, chocolate brown, and her head shaved. Her eyes widened when she saw Pressley.

The enforcer released her cuffs and shoved her forward without a word. The black girl caught Pressley by the arm before she fell on her face, and the door swung shut behind them. "Hmm," the girl said. "Come with me." She helped Pressley over to a soft, cream-colored sofa, moving slowly to accommodate Pressley's limp, and eased her down onto the cushions. "Wait here."

Pressley leaned back and closed her eyes. Her impression from what little she'd seen of the place was that of a smaller, shabbier cousin to the penthouse down the hall with windows set high in the walls, letting in light, but too high up to offer any view of the outside. Now that she had a soft seat and didn't seem to be in immediate danger, the pain of her injuries redoubled. Tears leaked out of her closed eyelids.

"Here."

Pressley opened her eyes. The black girl was back, carrying a load of first aid supplies in her arms. She dumped them onto a cushion and sat down beside Pressley. "Pain killers." She held them out on her palm. Pressley took them and gratefully popped them in her mouth. They fizzed pleasantly with a peachy flavor as they dissolved on her tongue. The girl applied a cold patch to Pressley's sore knee and another to her temple.

"I have some ointment for those welts if you don't mind lifting your shirt."

Pressley scooted forward and pulled the shirt off over her head. That was easier than trying to hold it up, and no one else seemed to be around. The girl spread the soothing ointment onto Pressley's welts with her long, delicate fingers and a gentle touch.

"You should be a nurse," Pressley said.

"I wish." Then even quieter, "Who did this to you?"

"Enforcer."

"Mm-hmm. They can be rough."

Pressley's blood froze at the implications of that.

"Not usually this rough, though. Can you stand up?"

"It was an interrogation," Pressley said while the girl deftly spread ointment beneath her flowery skirt. Thinking of the strip search, though, Pressley figured the girl's assumptions might not be too far off. "I didn't tell him anything," she said with a sudden burst of pride.

"All done. Is that better?"

"Much better." Pressley faced the girl. "Thank you."

"Here's a clean shirt if you want. I think it'll fit."

Pressley accepted the plain black top and pulled it over her welts and bruises, wincing only a little.

"There's a bathroom where you can wash up," the girl said. "But don't wash off the ointment yet."

"Okay." Pressley found the bathroom just down the hall and used a washcloth to remove the puke and blood as much as possible. She found the girl waiting for her on the couch. "I'm Olivia," she said.

"Pressley."

"I wish I could say I'm glad you're here."

A door banged open down the hall, and a pink-haired girl in a Hello Kitty t-shirt burst wide-eyed into the room. "Press?"

"Twiggy?"

Twiggy launched herself into Pressley's arms. Pressley grunted at the aggravation of her injuries, but she didn't let go. "Twiggy, I'm so sorry."

"You're Twiggy's sister?" Olivia asked.

Pressley nodded, still holding Twiggy tight. She'd switched off her holo-tat. The butterfly gleamed quietly on her neck.

"I thought you were dead," Twiggy sobbed into her chest. "I thought Ransom McCleary had you executed or something."

"Not yet," Pressley muttered into her hair.

Twiggy lifted her head, sniffling. "They said you stole something from him. That I had to stay until they got it back."

"I'm so sorry, Twiggy. I never meant for you to be involved."

"What did you steal?" Olivia asked, a question laced with anger.

"Data." Pressley sank back onto the couch. Twiggy sat beside her, and Pressley kept her arm around her sister. "I hacked into the Span Corp system and stole McCleary's personal files. I found…well, a lot of stuff, including a video. A recording of him murdering someone."

Twiggy lifted her head off Pressley's shoulder. "You're kidding."

Pressley shook her head. "I wish I was. But he killed a girl. Beat her to death." She finished in a whisper.

"The girl," Olivia asked in a hush. "What did she look like?"

Pressley's gut soured. "She was Asian. Petite and very pretty. Shoulder-length hair."

Olivia's face crumpled. "Shay." She collapsed onto the couch. "Oh, Shay." Her hands trembled.

"I'm sorry." Pressley wanted to do something to comfort the young woman but wasn't sure what Olivia wanted or needed. "So sorry," she said again, lamely. Like that would help anything.

"I kept telling myself that she was okay. That McCleary was keeping her all to himself or that she found a way to escape." She buried her face in her hands.

Twiggy leaned in closer to Pressley's side.

"Have they harmed you, Twig? Have they done anything to you?"

Twiggy's eyes widened. She shook her head and wrapped her arm around Pressley's waist like a child seeking comfort. Pressley squeezed her shoulders. "How many of you are up here?" Did she even want to know?

"A lot," Twiggy whispered.

Olivia brushed her hands across her eyes and stood. She clapped her hands. "Check-in time!"

A clattering of footsteps erupted in the hallway. Three young women came in, followed by two little girls and four teenage boys. Pressley sucked in a breath through her teeth.

"Everyone, this is Pressley. She's Twiggy's sister."

"Pressley, this is everyone." Olivia indicated the group. They stared at her without speaking, some with sympathy on their faces, others curiously or with apathy.

"She's kinda old," one of the little girls said, breaking the awkwardness. She wasn't wrong. Pressley was easily the oldest one here. And was it pregnancy giving her all these maternal, protective feelings?

"Maybe," Olivia said, "but she's here now, so be nice."

"I will." The little girl looked away.

"Good. Now, who's got dinner tonight?"

One of the boys raised his hand. "I do."

"Me too." That was one of the young women.

"Better get started." They all scattered, some to the kitchen to prep for dinner, some back to wherever they'd come from. The remaining boys plopped onto the couch and turned on a baseball game. The whole scene was so achingly homey it broke her heart.

"I need a phone," Pressley whispered.

Olivia snorted. "Don't we all. No phones in here."

"Any connection to the Span Corp system will do."

Olivia shook her head.

"We have to get you out of here."

"You can't get out of here. None of us can." Olivia's face grew hard. "You just put that notion out of your head right now, okay?"

"No, listen—"

"I know it's hard at first, but that's the way it is. The only way out of this place is the way Shay—" Her voice broke. She stood up. "Excuse me. I need a minute alone." She fled down the hall.

Twiggy tugged Pressley over to a private corner of the room. "I can't stay here. I just can't." Tears gathered in her blue eyes.

"I know, Twig." She leaned her forehead against Twiggy's. She leaned to whisper in Twiggy's ear. "I'm going to have a baby."

Twiggy gasped. "That's great." Her smile fell. "But not if we can't get away. McCleary won't let you carry it."

Well—that was true even as his employee.

"Olivia said we all get sterilized." Twiggy kept her voice quiet. "What are we going to do?"

"We have a plan," Pressley said, too low for the others to hear. "I just need to contact Mom and Malcolm.

"Mom?" Twiggy's forehead creased. "And who is Malcolm?"

"Malcolm is Mom's husband. Our stepfather."

"Our what?" Her voice rose, and the boys watching baseball looked over curiously. She lowered her volume. "Stepfather?"

"Yes. He's some ex-military action hero Mom met at church."

"I—wow. But…how do you know him?"

Pressley sighed. "I went home. I thought the enforcers wouldn't find me there, but they did."

Twiggy crinkled her nose. "I'm confused."

Pressley put her arm around her sister and leaned in close. "We came to L.A. to rescue you."

"Mom came?"

"Yes."

"She's here?"

"Yes. And we have a plan, like I said. Or we did. It's gone a little sideways, but if I can get in touch with them and access the computer system, we can still pull it off."

Maybe. If Mom and Malcolm hadn't been taken by the enforcers. If Malcolm could call in all his favors. She hadn't counted on being held captive at the top of this over-bloated tower—nor had she planned on how many people they'd have to rescue.

"I don't know, Press. Olivia's right. There are no phones. No contact with the outside."

Pressley considered the boys on the couch. The television would be connected to the Span Corp system somehow. There might be a way in for her there. She'd have to investigate further. And after all, she'd come this far against the odds. She had found Twiggy.

"I'm not giving up yet," she said. "Don't you give up either."

o o o

After a dinner Pressley could not eat, she approached Olivia again. Olivia's eyes were swollen and reddened, but she hadn't said anything about Shay to the others.

"Can I talk to you privately?"

"Okay." She led Pressley down the hall to one of the bedrooms and sat down on the end of the bed. Pressley sat beside her. Her welts were beginning to sting again, and the cold patches had dulled to room temperature. She peeled off the one stuck to her temple and tossed it aside. Her sore knee throbbed.

"I can't give you more pain meds yet," Olivia said. "Don't ask."

"I won't." She hesitated, then, "I'm pregnant."

"I'm sorry."

"I'm not." Irritation rose in her throat.

"Just forget it, okay?" Olivia said harshly. "From this moment on, you're not pregnant. You never will be. The sooner you accept that, the easier it'll be. Trust me."

Pressley shook her head. "I can't do that. But I can get us out of here. I can get justice for your friend. I just need to get access to the computer system."

"No!" Olivia came to her feet, blazing. "If you try anything, he'll know. He'll punish us all." Her eyes held some haunting memory, and Pressley could only imagine what she'd been through. "I won't allow it," Olivia insisted. "Please do yourself a favor and forget your old life right now. Outside these walls, we don't exist, but in here, we're family. And I won't let you endanger my family."

What about my family? "You don't understand. We have a plan in place—"

"No!" Her fierceness took Pressley back. "It won't work. Believe me. I don't want to hear any more about it."

Pressley's jaw tightened.

Olivia's expression turned sorrowful. "I'm sorry you're here. Wouldn't wish it on anyone. But we'll take care of you, I promise." Her voice dropped to a whisper. Was she thinking of her friend Shay?

Sickness rose in Pressley's throat. How many others had simply disappeared like Shay?

"You're the new girl. You get clean-up duty."

"Clean-up duty?"

"Clean up the kitchen, wash the dishes, do the floors, start the laundry." She shrugged. "Easy."

Olivia turned away, her shoulders slumped. Pressley wanted to comfort her, but what could she say? She didn't say anything. Olivia hurried away.

Twiggy came back into the room. "What are you doing? What did Olivia say?"

"I'm on clean-up."

"You want help?" Twiggy asked.

"Sure."

The kitchen and dining room were an unholy mess. The kids in charge of dinner had dirtied everything in sight. Pressley had to stand with her hand over her nose and mouth for several seconds before getting started.

Twiggy cleared the table, piling dishes up on the counter. They seemed to have been accumulating all day. Clearly, the little dishwasher wouldn't hold much. Pressley ran hot water into the sink, adding dish soap and watching the bubbles foam.

"Get as much as you can into the dishwasher," she told Twiggy.

"You didn't tell me what Olivia said."

"She said we'll never get out of here, and if we try, we'll all be punished. And that we all take care of each other in here."

"So that's it, then?"

"I didn't say that."

"What about school? My acting career? It isn't fair."

"No." Pressley plunged a pan into the soapy water. "It isn't fair. Not to you. Not to the others." Not to Bobby or Mom or Malcolm. So much in this city and everywhere else just wasn't fair. She attacked the pan like she wanted to scrub a hole in the bottom.

"What kinds of electronic devices do they have in here?" she asked quietly. "Does anyone have a phone?"

"Nope. The enforcers took mine."

"Me too."

"The little girls have kids' tablets. I think there are some e-readers too."

"Okay. I might be able to work with that."

"Really?" Twiggy's voice rose in hopeful anticipation.

"Maybe. It's a long shot, but all I need is to get into Span Corp's system."

"You have to get us out of here, Press."

"Shhh. I know. I'll have to try it when Olivia isn't around."

"She'll probably be gone later." Twiggy caught Pressley's eyes over the dirty dishes, her expression haunted. "Most of them will."

Pressley nodded, feeling sick again. They finished the dishes, swept and mopped the floors, sorted a staggering amount of laundry in the small laundry room off the kitchen, and got the washer started.

Exhausted, Pressley collapsed onto a dining room chair and buried her head in her hands. After a couple of minutes, Twiggy touched her shoulder.

"There are still too many people around. I can't find an unused tablet for you." She bounced a little on her toes.

"That's okay. We can wait until everyone's asleep."

Twiggy gave her a pained look. She thumped her fist against her thigh.

"Be patient. I'm not even sure this will work."

That clearly wasn't the right thing to say. Twiggy turned the color of curdled cream. Her holo-tat glimmered starkly against her neck.

Pressley stood and pulled her close. "Don't worry. I'm here to watch out for you."

"I'm scared."

"I know," Pressley whispered. She was afraid too. "I bet Mom's praying for us." Mom was always praying.

"Yeah? Maybe."

"She misses you a lot."

Twiggy was silent.

"Come on," Pressley said. "I could use a shower. Think you can find me some clean clothes?"

"Yeah, okay." Twiggy trotted off, leaving Pressley alone. She found the bathroom unoccupied and got in the shower. The water stung the welts on her back, but the ointment Olivia had used tempered the pain. The hot water felt wonderful, washing away the lingering smell of the vomit and easing her aches.

She finished washing and turned off the water, leaning her head against the tile. Weariness settled into her bones. Were Mom and Malcolm waiting to hear from her? Was Bobby wondering if she was okay? Or did they think she was dead?

She moaned softly. Would she ever see Bobby or her parents again? Would she ever give birth to the baby inside her or walk free in the sunshine again?

With a shiver, Pressley straightened and wiped the tears from her face. She dried off and dressed in the faded lounge pants and ratty purple tank Twiggy had left on the vanity.

Her sister waited just outside the bathroom door, twisting a hot pink pigtail around one finger. "Still some kids awake."

"We might as well get some rest," Pressley said. "Show me where I can sleep."

"You can share my bed." Twiggy linked her arm through Pressley's and led her into a bedroom with two sets of bunk beds. Twiggy tugged her up to the top bunk on one side. Like a small child, she snuggled up against Pressley's side, grabbed her hand, and wouldn't let go. Pressley wrapped a protective arm around her and fell quickly asleep.

When she awoke, the alarm clock on the little nightstand read 3:10. Twiggy breathed softly and evenly beside her. Below, Olivia sniffled quietly. Pressley's heart ached.

She waited silently until Olivia's crying gave way to sounds of sleeping. Then she sneaked quietly out of bed and relieved her overactive bladder. That would make for a good excuse if anyone wanted to know why she was up in the middle of the night.

She tiptoed into the little girls' bedroom. They were both asleep in their own bunk, tiny lumps under the covers. Pressley crept to a charging bin attached to the wall and retrieved one of the tablets inside.

One of the girls stirred when the tablets clanked a bit. She sat up in bed.

"Sorry," Pressley whispered and hurried out. She stood in the hallway, listening for a minute, but heard nothing. She went into the living room and curled her legs up under herself on a corner of the couch with all the lights off.

It was a Span Corp tablet, of course. It didn't have Wi-Fi, only some games and educational programs. But they were Span Corp apps, and with a little digging, she found that, as she suspected, they were connected to the in-house Span Corp system.

Perfect.

A few minutes later, she was back in. A quick check revealed the video was ready to post, and she still had access to the data siphon.

Now she needed a way to contact Mom and Malcolm and Bobby in a manner that wouldn't arouse suspicion if they—or their phones, anyway—were compromised. Oh, man. She hoped they weren't. With a little finagling, she reenabled the tablet's Wi-Fi. Now to compose a message.

"What are you doing?"

Pressley jumped. She hadn't noticed Olivia coming into the room.

"Where did you get that?" she shrieked.

Pressley held the tablet against her chest. "From the charging bin."

"Give it to me."

"No."

Olivia lunged across the room. Pressley scrambled off the couch out of her way, hampered by the pain in her knee and the nausea clutching her stomach.

"I told you! I told you what will happen. You'll get us all in trouble! You'll get us all killed!"

"Stop, Olivia. Listen to me." Pressley backpedaled, holding the tablet over her head, out of reach. But Olivia didn't stop or listen. She plowed into Pressley. They both went down. Pressley's head banged against the floor. The tablet went skidding. Olivia clawed her way over Pressley to get at it.

"No! Give it back to me." Pressley struggled to get up. Olivia charged down the hall. Lights came on in the bedrooms, and surprised faces poked out of the doors.

Pressley hustled after Olivia as fast as she could on her aching knee. Olivia slapped a panel on the wall and a staircase lowered from a trap door in the ceiling. Pressley caught up as the stairs finished lowering. She grabbed Olivia's shoulder. "Please."

Olivia elbowed her hard in the gut. Pressley grunted and doubled over, stumbling back a step or two. Twiggy was there to steady her. Seemed the whole house was awake now.

Olivia took the stairs two at a time. Pressley couldn't go as fast but wasn't far behind. A skylight washed the nearly empty attic in soft moonlight and neon glow. Olivia shouldered aside an old queen-size mattress, leaning against the wall to uncover a small metal door. She hit a button and the door slid aside, revealing the roof of Span Corp tower.

Pressley's breath caught as she realized Olivia's intention. She clenched her teeth and ignored the pain, lunged forward, caught hold of Olivia, and dragged her back from the short railing dotted with warning lights, the only barrier between the rooftop and the long, long drop to the street below.

"Don't throw it off. I need that."

Olivia struggled in her arms. Pressley held on tight. "Give me the tablet," she said.

"No!"

"Please just hear me out."

"No!"

Olivia continued to thrash. Pressley dragged them both to the ground like some kind of MMA fighter. "I'm trying to help you!" she grunted.

"Whoa. Whoa. Whoa." Two of the boys tried to drag them apart while Twiggy attempted to pry the tablet away from Olivia.

"I got it!" Twiggy crowed.

Pressley relaxed her hold and fell back onto the rooftop. The boys helped Olivia up.

"What is this about?" one of them asked. Pressley thought his name was Jaden.

Twiggy had the tablet clutched up against her chest. Everyone was on the roof now, staring in astonishment at the scene.

"She's going to get us all killed!" Olivia screamed.

"No, I'm not." Pressley pulled herself up. "I'm going to get justice for Shay. For all of you."

"Where's Shay?" one of the little girls, Bess, asked, her voice small in the vast night. Sounds of traffic and jets, music and advertising, the soundtrack of life in L.A., swallowed up her little voice, but the question hung heavily in the air.

Olivia's breathing grew harsh and ragged. "Shay is dead," she said, hot and sharp as a switchblade. The little girl started to cry. "Ransom McCleary killed her with his own hands."

Someone let out an anguished moan.

"I have the evidence," Pressley said. "Evidence that he can't cover up or weasel out of. The cops will have to arrest him."

"And he'll send his enforcers in to kill us as soon as that happens," Olivia said.

"I can get us out of here. I have people waiting to rescue us."

"Us?" another of the boys asked.

"Twiggy and me. But they can get the rest of you too. I just need to contact them. They're waiting to hear from me."

"Knights in shining armor?" Olivia asked scornfully.

"My family." She explained the plan to all of them, not leaving out the fact that her rescuers might also have been caught by the enforcers. "But I feel hopeful they were able to get away."

"That's a pretty thin hope," Olivia said.

"But it is hope." Twiggy pressed the tablet tight against her chest. "There is hope, isn't there, Press?"

"I wouldn't be trying it if I thought there wasn't any hope."

"Let's take a vote," Jaden said. "You can't decide this for us, Olivia."

Olivia was quiet for a few seconds, her face tight with emotion. "Fine," she said finally. "All in favor?"

Twiggy's arm rocketed up. The others considered, and more hands went up. Only Olivia and the youngest of the boys, Carter, disagreed. Jaden nudged Carter with his elbow. He grumbled and lifted his hand.

Olivia folded her arms. "You all really want to risk this?"

"For Shay," one of the young women said.

"For us," Jaden added.

"All right, then." Olivia walked to the edge of the rooftop and wrapped her hands around the railing.

Pressley looked around her for the first time. The vista from up here was stunning, dizzying. The roof was about twenty meters on each side, and the walls of the attic space jutted up behind them in a small wedge. On top of that was a tall lightning rod with a warning light blinking on top. The city spread out beneath them, aglow in the hour before dawn. A restless breeze blew off the ocean. The whining of drones and distant buzzing of airplanes colored the air.

"Why didn't you tell us about this place, Liv?" the older girl asked.

"It was our secret. Shay and me. We used to come up here and dream about our future. As if we had one."

"We should stay up here," Bess said. "It's kind of like a hiding place."

"Yeah, in case he does send enforcers for us."

"It won't take them very long to find the door in the attic." Olivia faced them again.

"But it might be long enough," Pressley said.

Bess smiled. Olivia still looked a little sullen.

Pressley gently touched Olivia's shoulder. "Maybe long enough to ensure you have a future."

"Maybe." Olivia met her eyes. "All right. For Shay. Let's do it, then."

With dawn approaching, they made their preparations. They gathered up what belongings they wanted to take with them into backpacks and totes. It wasn't much. Pressley took a paring knife with a hard, plastic cover from a kitchen drawer and put it in her pocket. It wasn't much of a weapon, but it was something.

Half an hour later, they all emerged onto the rooftop again. The rising sun painted the sky a dull pink.

With some difficulty, Pressley, Olivia, and two of the boys managed to wrangle the mattress back in front of the door from the outside. It looked ready to topple over, but when Olivia shut the door, they heard no sound of it falling. Unfortunately, they had no way of locking the door or barricading it from the outside.

The little group sat close together, away from the attic door and away from the edge of the roof. They spoke in hushed voices, though once in a while a laugh would erupt out of the quiet, and the offending party would quickly be shushed.

Pressley sat apart from the rest. A cool breeze off the sea ruffled her hair. She opened the tablet and set to work. They'd soon find out if all this was worth it. If Ransom McCleary would pay for his crimes. She accessed the Span Corp messaging system, which would allow her to post the video on every Span Corp-owned phone in the world.

But first, she had to get a message to Bobby or Malcolm or both, if—*Please, God*—they were still alive. Still free.

She composed a message that she hoped would seem random and meaningless if they or their phones were compromised but that they would understand if they got it.

Hey, party on the rooftop in 30 after the film premiere. Just me and T and like ten others. Please come. I miss you.

She sent it to both of them with the dummy phone number she'd set up, hoping that one or both of them would see it, understand, and find some way to come for them.

She queued up the video in the messaging system and set it to start in thirty minutes. Then she did the same with all the Span Corp-run video projectors. Her finger trembled over the timer.

"Thirty minutes to showtime," she whispered and hit the button.

The quiet of dawn on the rooftop seemed anti-climactic. Jaden stood up to pace. Olivia held onto the railing, staring out over the cityscape. Airplanes and drones crisscrossed overhead. Twiggy leaned against Pressley. "I can't believe you went back to Mom's. She must have been pissed about you being pregnant and all. Or did you even tell her?"

"I did tell her, and she wasn't mad. She was happy about it."

"Our mother? Are you sure it was really her?"

Pressley laughed. "Yes. Really her. I think marriage chilled her out. And the fact that she's pregnant too."

Twiggy sat up and punched her in the arm. "No, she's not."

"She is." Pressley rubbed the spot without complaining. She didn't want to remind Twiggy she'd just been stripped and beaten by the same enforcers who might be coming for all of them in a few minutes.

"I don't think I want to see Mom again," Twiggy said quietly. "No matter how much she's chilled."

Pressley nodded. "I know. But she wants to see you. She risked everything to come out here and rescue you." And for all they knew, she may have lost everything too. "I just hope she's still alive."

"Yeah." Twiggy sighed. "Me too."

They sat for a few more minutes in silence, Pressley trying hard not to second-guess herself. It was too late to turn back now.

Eventually, Olivia left the rail and sat cross-legged beside Pressley and Twiggy.

"When it starts," Pressley told her, "don't watch it."

"I owe it to Shay to see what happened."

"No. She wouldn't want you to have to live with that sight. Trust me."

Carter came to join them, pushing his overgrown hair out of his face. "You just posted a video for the whole world that you don't want anyone to see?"

"Yes. I wish I didn't have to, but I did. I had to ensure the cops or whoever I showed it to didn't just sweep it under the rug." She thought of Hazard Snow and her jaw tightened. "McCleary can't claim it is a fake, either. Any phone can verify it hasn't been tampered with."

Olivia sighed. "Can you tell me why? Why did he kill her?"

Pressley considered her answer carefully. "It looked to me like she said something. Something that made McCleary angry."

"Oh, Shay. She always did have such a mouth on her—never knew when to keep it shut, either." She lowered her head.

"We'll make him pay."

"My fellow citizens—" Malcolm's voice boomed out over the building—a warning they'd added to the video at Mother's insistence.

Showtime.

Olivia's head bobbed up, her eyes wide.

"My name is Malcolm Burke. I am a former Marine and decorated veteran of the Red Moon War.

The video you are about to see is a real recording of a real murder perpetrated by one of the most powerful men in the world.

"What you are about to see is graphic and disturbing. Please remove small children and sensitive persons from the viewing area, or avert your eyes."

A moment of quiet followed. Pressley imagined with some satisfaction Span Corp's cyber-security team trying and failing to shut the video down. They'd never get through her firewalls in time.

The muffled sounds of Ransom McCleary's unthinkable act began. Olivia's expression grew more horrified. The others looked around nervously. A couple of them came to their feet. Pressley motioned them over to her. "Don't watch. It's awful." They gathered into a tight circle. The little girls held hands. From the video came a cry of pain. Twiggy winced as if she were the one being struck.

Olivia jumped up, her eyes wild. She ran to the edge of the roof, leaning over the railing to watch the scene play out on the buildings below, all across the city. "No," Pressley came to her feet too. Olivia screamed Shay's name, her voice raw. Pressley ran—or more like quickly hobbled—to her, fearing she'd throw herself off the edge in her grief.

"Olivia." She touched her arm. "Don't watch it."

Olivia looked at her but didn't seem to see her. Her eyes were wild, feral. Her hands clutched the railing tight enough to leave indentations in the metal.

"I'll kill him," she said hoarsely through her teeth. "I'll kill him with my bare hands."

"I know." Pressley felt sick again, trying desperately to tear her eyes away. The sight was so much worse plastered larger than life above the city. She should never have done it. Olivia and the others did not deserve such pain.

"I'm so sorry."

But Olivia didn't hear her. An anguished bellow tore from her throat into the bitter morning. She slumped to the floor, her face in her hands. One of the other girls hurried over to comfort her while Pressley stood by helplessly.

The screens went blank, and Malcolm's voice resonated over the city again. "I call for the immediate arrest of Ransom McCleary and anyone who has aided his coverup of this heinous crime."

The video faded out. Pressley wrapped her arms around her tummy, not wanting to puke on the rooftop or, God forbid, over the edge onto some poor, unsuspecting sap hundreds of feet below.

Twiggy came toward her. "What now?"

"Shh." Jaden put a finger to his lips. "I hear something."

The city was full of noises—traffic, honking, sirens, drones overhead, bits of music, the ads, and other vids playing on the sides of the buildings again now that her intrusion had played out.

But it wasn't any of that Jaden was referring to. Pressley slipped the paring knife from the kitchen out of her pocket. She heard it too. Banging and thumping from below them. "They're coming."

"Our rescue party?" Twiggy asked, but Pressley doubted Malcolm or Bobby could have found them so quickly. And they'd still have to get through the enforcers. No. Their hiding place had been discovered.

"Get out of sight of the door," Pressley said. The only option was next to the wall jutting up from the attic. That would keep them hidden for all of two seconds. Hopefully, that would be enough.

She motioned Jaden to the side of the door. "Get ready. I'll stab him and you get his gun."

"Got it."

He was only a skinny teenage boy, not a cyber-enhanced enforcer. She had nothing but a paring knife. The banging grew louder. Heavy footsteps in the attic. The sound of someone shoving the mattress aside.

Pressley readied herself. Adrenaline covered her aches. Jaden's eyes were wide with fear as he crouched on the other side of the door, ready to spring. His breath came hard and fast. Pressley gave him a grim nod.

The door opened.

Pressley stabbed. The knife sank into the bicep of the enforcer. He howled in pain. Pressley sliced upward through the muscles. Despite the injury, the enforcer swung his arm with force and sent her flying backward. Her head cracked against the rooftop.

Blackness covered her vision for a second or two. She pushed herself up, wobbly and queasy, in time to see Jaden fire the enforcer's gun. The shot went wide as the kick threw the skinny boy backward onto his butt so close to the railing Pressley was afraid he'd go right over.

The others sent up a chorus of screaming. Pressley ran for Jaden, but her knee wouldn't work, and her vision turned sideways. The enforcer was coming for Jaden too, blood dripping from his arm and fury from his face. Another armed enforcer crashed through the door behind him.

Jaden fired the gun again from his sitting position and toppled backward. Pressley screamed. He managed to wrap a hand around the railing and avoid going right off the edge. The enforcer fell dead. Lucky shot.

The second enforcer raised his rifle. He seemed to hesitate, deciding whether to shoot Jaden or Pressley or the panicked group behind him. Pressley staggered forward, unsure what she even intended to do—stab him? She seemed to have dropped the paring knife. Her thoughts kept sliding around each other and away from her.

The enforcer settled on Jaden. Pressley lunged. Her knee gave out again. She was too far away to do anything anyway.

The enforcer's head shattered into fragments of brain, machinery, and bone. Pressley collapsed to her hands and knees and vomited, and somehow Bobby was there beside her.

"Press, are you okay? Are you hurt? You're bleeding!"

She became aware of cops spilling out from the attic, Mom and Malcolm behind them. Bobby motioned to the EMTs coming out with stretchers. Pressley leaned against him. Darkness encroached on her vision again. "Did they get him? Did they get McCleary?" She couldn't hold herself up any longer. Bobby's arms closed around her as she sagged.

"Yes," he said, or she thought he did. None of it was quite clear. "Yes, they got him."

There were more words, but she didn't understand them, except her mother's voice saying, "Stay with us, Pressley. Hang on, baby girl."

EPILOGUE

A few wispy clouds spread across the sky over an equally blue, serene sea. Olivia played with the little girls, dancing in and out of the waves at the water's edge. Bess and Lila's new foster mother hovered nearby, a nervous mother hen. A few seagulls flew overhead, and more hopped across the sand, fighting over scraps of food.

Pressley stretched out her legs and reclined in the beach chair. She ran her hand over the taut skin of her swollen belly. The baby squirmed inside her. A tiny foot stretched out as if to meet her hand. Not long now until she'd hold him in her arms. That day couldn't come soon enough for her. She wasn't sure what would happen after that. Mother had suggested starting a cybersecurity consulting business. Not a bad idea. But whatever she decided, at least she had the freedom to choose her future for herself.

Her phone chimed with an incoming text. She thought it would be from Bobby, but it was from Corny.

Any baby news?

She smiled. *Not yet, but you'll be one of the first to know.*

Good. Cuz this little guy's gotta get to know his Uncle Corny.

Yes, he does. He will. I promise. Love you, Corny. Thanks for everything. You made a big difference for us.

You did too, Press. I mean that. A huge difference. Love you, too.

Olivia left the little girls splashing each other and sat down in the sand next to Pressley. "Any news?"

"Not yet." Not from Bobby at the trial or from Twiggy at her first real audition or Malcolm at the farmstead with Mom—though Olivia probably wasn't as interested in Mom's impending delivery or Twiggy's audition as she was in the outcome of Ransom McCleary's trial.

"I'm scared," Olivia whispered.

"No way he's getting off." She touched Olivia's shoulder. Her baby wriggled inside her again. "Not after your testimony—and the others. That was really brave of you."

"But if he does get off—"

"He won't. Look—" She pointed to where Bobby came traipsing across the beach toward them. He wore the suit Hazard Snow had bought for him, ironically enough, with the pants rolled up around his calves and his feet bare. He carried his nice wingtips in one hand.

Bess and Lila noticed and came running toward them, sand coating their little feet. Their foster mom trailed close behind. Olivia stood up, but Pressley stayed in her beach chair. Getting up at this point was too monumental an effort.

"Guilty," Bobby announced. "On all counts. Ransom McCleary is going to prison for the rest of his life."

Bess and Lila cheered. Olivia stood speechless. Her chin quivered. A lone tear spilled down her cheek. Pressley couldn't stay seated seeing that. She beckoned for Bobby to help get her out of the lounge chair. Upright at last, she pulled Olivia into a tight embrace. Hot tears wet Pressley's neck. "He can't hurt you ever again."

Olivia lifted her head. "Thanks to you."

"I'm just glad they got him." And that she'd saved Twiggy and that Hazard Snow had been forced to drop out of the governor's race and testify against McCleary in a plea deal.

"I just wish Shay were here to see him go to jail."
Olivia shuddered.

"We all do. But you will honor her memory best by living a full and happy life. Becoming a nurse and helping many, many others."

Olivia nodded and brushed away her tears. "You really think I can?"

"I know you can. You're already on your way."

Olivia smiled through her tears. "Thank you." She drew in her breath. "Good luck with your baby."

"I'll let you know when he arrives."

"Can we come see him?" Bess asked.

"Yes, of course. I hope you do."

"It's time to go," the foster mom announced. "Come rinse your feet off. Olivia, you still want to catch a ride with us?"

"Yes, please."

After a flurry of hugs and goodbyes, Pressley and Bobby stood alone on the sand. She took his hand, letting the steady rhythm of the waves quiet the stuttering of her heart. She'd done it. Brought down Ransom McCleary and Hazard Snow. Opened the way for important changes. She'd saved her sister and the others. She expected to feel more satisfied, but despite being all full of a wiggly baby with hiccups, she felt rather empty.

"You did good," Bobby said like maybe he knew what she was feeling.

"You weren't so bad yourself, saving our lives and all." She bumped her shoulder against his.

"Just trying to protect my family. That's what fathers do, right?"

"So I've been told."

"Press—" He took her other hand, looking into her eyes with an intensity that left her suddenly breathless—or maybe that was the baby pressing on her diaphragm.

"A few months ago, all I cared about was surfing and making love to you."

She smiled. The wind tousled his bleached-blond hair.

"And I still care about those things. But ever since you told me you were pregnant, everything changed."

"Understatement of the year."

"Yeah, and now what I want most is to take care of you and our baby. Our family."

The baby kicked again, making her tummy jump. "He can hear you."

"Good." He rested his hand on the swell of her belly. "I know I don't have a lot to offer right now, but I'm working on it."

She couldn't argue with that. He'd been working hard for Malcolm as a farm hand and still making deliveries on the side.

"And I'll keep working hard," he said. He threaded his fingers through hers. "And if I can still go surfing sometimes, great. And if I can still make love to you, even better."

A laugh bubbled out of her. Her chest warmed. The emptiness receded a little.

Bobby dropped to one knee, and suddenly she couldn't breathe.

"Pressley, will you marry me?"

Out of a pocket of his suit he pulled a diamond ring, glittering like a miniature star on his outstretched palm.

"Where did you get that?" She picked it up and admired its elegant lines. Tears began to prick at her eyes.

"I got it yesterday from a guy I Uber for. Been saving up."

"It's so beautiful." Her throat tightened.

Bobby stood. "Is that a yes?"

Pressley nodded, not trusting her voice anymore.

Bobby slipped the ring onto her finger. "I love you, Press. I will forever."

She wrapped her arms around him, and he kissed her under the warm sun. The sea crashed beyond them.

The gulls cried overhead. The baby moved between them.

Maybe this would work out after all.

THE END

About the Author

Angie Lofthouse went to college with every intention of becoming a particle physicist, but through a series of misadventures, found herself studying Shakespeare instead. After college she combined her love of science and her love of words into a science fiction writing career.

She is the author of Defenders of the Covenant, The Ransomed Returning, and The Glory of the Stars, as well as numerous short stories and novellas.

She lives in a little canyon in the foothills of the Wasatch Mountains with her family and enjoys strumming her ukulele, watching baseball, and playing with her grandchildren. You can find her on Instagram and YouTube.

Acknowledgements

A heartfelt thanks goes out to beta readers Tracy Lofthouse, Suzette Saxton, and Mandi Ellsworth for reading early drafts and offering invaluable suggestions. A huge thanks also goes to Adrienne Quintana and Marnae Kelley of Pink Umbrella Books for their excellent work with editing, formatting, and cover design. I couldn't have done it without you!